BATTA

BLACKWINGS
DEVIL SPRINGS

TEAGAN
BROOKS

BATTA

BLACKWINGS MC - DEVIL SPRINGS - BOOK FOUR

TEAGAN BROOKS

CONTENTS

Adult Content Warning: This book is intended for readers 18 years old and older due to sexual content, explicit language, and violence.

ACKNOWLEDGMENTS

Cover Design: C.T. Cover Creations

Cover Model: Hank Meyer

Cover Photographer: FuriousFotog

Proofreading and Copyediting: Kathleen Martin

Content and Developmental Editing: Rogue Readers

Special thanks to Kathleen Martin, Melissa Rivera, Tina Workman, Jennifer Ritch, Jenna Sage, Katherine Smith, Brittany Franks, Courtney Lynn Rose, and Jamie Hensley.

To my Guinness.

I miss you.

NOTE FROM THE AUTHOR

Trey is a common nickname for the third person in a family to have the same name. Batta's name in Jace Ryder Wild III, but he went by Trey until he was given his road name.

PROLOGUE

BATTA

Thirteen Years Ago

"Mom, I'm going out with Copper, Bronze, and Jonah," I called as I headed out the door.

"Just a minute," she called out as she quickly walked down the hall. "You boys behave yourselves. Call me or one of the other moms if you need a ride home." She'd been saying those exact words to me every time I left the house on a Friday or Saturday night since I started high school.

"We will. I promise."

"Good," she said and wrapped her arms around my waist. "I love you."

Since I'd long outgrown her, I held her against my chest and kissed the top of her head. "I love you, too, Mom."

"Your dad called a little while ago. He'll be home in a few hours, so I'm going to go over to Sarah's and watch a movie with her. I left a note for him on the kitchen table, but he might not see it, so let him know if he calls you."

Sarah was our next-door neighbor. When she first moved in, she kept to herself; we didn't even know she was there for the first few months. Mom ran into her at the mailbox one day, and they'd been friends ever since. Something about the woman bothered me, but Dad was happy that Mom had a friend close by. Between his responsibilities for the club and his job, Dad was gone more often than he was home. Mom had friends in the club, particularly Goldie and Leigh, but both of them lived on the other side of town and Mom didn't like to drive at night.

"Have fun. We shouldn't be too late," I told her and hugged her once more before I left.

THE PARTY WE WENT TO WAS BORING AS HELL, SO we left and went back to Jonah's house and started a small bonfire in the backyard. We were about ready to call it a night when we heard bikes in the distance. A lot of bikes. And they were headed in our direction.

Jonah jumped up and took off toward the house in a full sprint. I completely froze when I was hit with a weird sense of déjà vu. The year before, the four of us were standing in the parking lot after school when we heard the rumble of multiple motorcycles approaching. That was the day Jonah's dad died.

Copper grabbed my shoulder and gave it a firm shake. "Come on, man. Something must be wrong."

His words were enough to get me moving and I followed him to the house. Leigh was in the kitchen pacing and wringing her hands. "I don't know anything. Hawk called and asked if you boys were here. As soon as I said yes, he told me not to let you leave and hung up."

"What do you think it is?" Jonah whispered.

"There's no sense in speculating. They'll be here in a few minutes and we'll know."

Those few minutes seemed like an eternity.

Copper and Bronze's dad, Hawk, came through the door with a grim look on his face. His officers were right behind him with matching expressions.

We were all frozen in place, anticipating the delivery of devastating news. And then his eyes landed on me. "Trey," he croaked and attempted to clear the emotion from his throat. "Have a seat, son."

I shook my head. "Tell me now. Mom or Dad?"

Hawk dropped his head and clenched his hands into fists. "Your mother."

"Is she…?" Bronze whispered.

"I'm sorry," Hawk rasped.

For a few seconds, everything stopped. My heart. My breath. My life. Then, it all came rushing back and hit me like a sledgehammer when Leigh's heart-wrenching scream filled the air.

My mother was gone.

Mom.

Dead.

The crushing pain in my chest was too much. I couldn't breathe. I needed air. I needed to get the fuck out of that room.

Jumping to my feet, I ran for the door. Copper

tried to stop me, but he was no match for the rage and hurt coursing through me. Shoving him out of the way, I ran for my truck and grabbed my bat from the bed. The next few minutes were a blur of wood swinging, glass breaking, and metal crushing as I roared like a wild beast into the night with each hit I landed. Tears blinded my vision, but the rage wanted out, so I kept swinging.

I could have continued beating the hell out of my truck, and anything else that got in front of me, for hours, because the anger was keeping the pain at bay. I don't know how long I went at it, but my bat finally splintered into useless pieces of wood, and I collapsed to the ground. Hawk dropped down beside me, wrapped his arms around me, and held me while the pain, anger, and complete devastation destroyed me. One by one, Copper, Bronze, and Jonah joined Hawk on the ground, and the four of them tried to hold me together.

"We've got you," Copper promised. "We've always got you."

They stayed with me until I could finally speak. "Dad?" I asked.

"We're trying to find him," Hawk told me.

"Does he know?"

"He does. He was the one who found her, and he was the one to call it in. He disappeared after the police arrived. We thought maybe he was on his way to you but realized that wasn't the case when we talked to Leigh."

"I don't know what to do," I confessed.

"The only thing you need to do right now is get in the car with my boys and come to the clubhouse. Jonah and Leigh are coming, too. The club will take care of everything else."

"Okay," I agreed dazedly. I felt like I was in a fog, and the pain where my heart used to be was trying to consume me. I couldn't even begin to make my body execute the most basic functions. My best friends, who were more like my brothers, helped me to my feet. With Copper on one side and Judge on the other, they carried me to the truck and climbed in the back with me, while Bronze drove us to the clubhouse. Then, they stayed by my side and held me up during the darkest time of my life.

DAYS PASSED, AND DAD WAS STILL MISSING. EVEN

though no one would say it, we all knew what he was doing; we just didn't know where he was doing it.

As it turned out, our new neighbor, Sarah, had an abusive husband she'd finally managed to get away from…until he found her. And my mother was caught in the crossfire. Sarah's husband kicked in the front door and shot my mother, killing her instantly. Sarah's death was not as quick, and it was much more horrifying.

My father disappeared the moment he learned who the main suspect was. Hell, the man didn't even try to hide his identity. He left the gun in the house along with fingerprints all over the place. The cops knew who they were looking for within thirty minutes of being on the scene.

The detectives hadn't been able to find a single trace of the man, and I had no doubt it was because my father found him first and was making him pay for killing my mother.

Three days after my world was shattered, my dad walked into the clubhouse and came straight for me. He wrapped me in a bear hug and told me how sorry he was. He asked me to make sure my mother's funeral would be as beautiful as she was. Then, he walked out the door and got on his bike.

Hours later, I learned that he rode straight to the police station and turned himself in for the murder of Sarah's husband. Since he spent three days torturing him in ways that made my skin crawl to even think about before he finally ended the man's life, all chances of pleading temporary insanity were gone.

Hawk's uncle, Tommy Black, was a lawyer and did everything he could to help. He didn't have a lot to work with, but he was able to get the charges reduced to second-degree murder. Even still, Dad was sentenced to twenty years in prison.

I never returned to the house where I grew up. I stayed at the clubhouse or with Jonah until Dad was sentenced. Then, I permanently moved in with Leigh and Jonah.

After losing my mother, my father, and the only home I ever knew, my entire world was shattered, and the entire course of my life was completely off track. All because a woman with secrets moved in next door.

PROLOGUE

TATUM

Two Months Ago

"I need help, Tatum," my sister whispered into the phone. "Right now." I could tell she was crying, but the blatant fear and panic in her voice sent chills down my spine.

"I'm on my way. Tell me what's going on," I instructed.

"You need to bring your friends and come now," she whispered. "I have to go."

"No! Josie, don't hang up!" I shouted, but she was already gone.

"Dave! Let's go," I yelled to my partner as I grabbed my keys. "Jack, you and Matt follow us."

Dave took the keys from my hand. "You tell me where we're going, and I'll drive."

"My sister's house," I said shakily. "I don't know what's wrong. She just said she needed help and that I should bring my friends." I took in a deep breath and tried to ignore the dread swelling inside me. "I've never heard her like that. She sounded…terrified."

On the way there, I drove myself crazy trying to figure out what could possibly be wrong. If it was a home invasion, she would've called 9-1-1, not me. I immediately discounted a domestic dispute as the reasoning. My sister's extremely wealthy husband was…disinterested at best. I never understood why she married him. They didn't seem to be in love, but she said she was happy and swore he was good to her. Personally, I thought he married her for appearances. Regardless of their reasoning, I couldn't complain; he spent a lot of time traveling for work, which meant I got to spend a lot of time with my sister.

My thoughts were interrupted minutes later

when we arrived at the mansion Sheldon bought right after he and Josie were married. I thought the place was an ostentatious eyesore, but my sister loved it; so, I kept my opinions to myself.

Dave pulled into the driveway, and I jumped out of the car before it completely came to a stop. "Tatum!" he hissed. "If you want to help your sister, you need to stop thinking with your heart and follow your training."

Fuck. He was right, but my sister was inside, and she needed me. In a very uncharacteristic move, I conceded. "You take the lead."

With guns drawn and ready, we approached the house and started to check the perimeter. The two gunshots that sounded from somewhere inside the house had me breaking protocol and running for the front door. With a burst of adrenaline, I opened the door with my booted foot and barreled inside.

I followed the sound of a scuffle to the partially open door that led to the basement. Just as I was about to open it fully, someone running up the stairs plowed into my chest and immediately began to fight against me.

With a brief glance at the small woman, I

dismissed her as a threat and shoved her out of my way so I could see what was going on in the basement.

I rushed down the stairs and stopped dead in my tracks. My sister and her husband were lying motionless on the floor as a pool of blood formed around them. Sheldon's injury was obvious, but I couldn't immediately see where Josie was hurt.

"Nooooooo!" I screamed. "No! Oh, please, no! Josie! I need help! Fuck! Somebody help me!" I wailed while I frantically tried to search my sister's body for a wound.

Large hands landed on my shoulders and tried to pull me away. "Let me help her," Dave said softly. "Go upstairs, Tatum. You don't need to see this."

"I'm not leaving her," I cried.

"That girl up there needs a woman to help her. Go!"

I twisted and shoved him away as hard as I could. "I'm not leaving her," I cried and didn't bother to wipe away the tears clouding my vision.

"Josie! Wake up!" I screamed and started to shake her limp body.

"Tatum!" Dave roared in a tone I'd never

heard from him before as Jack physically separated me from my sister. "Go upstairs!"

"No!" I yelled, kicking and thrashing against Jack.

Dave slapped his hands together millimeters from my nose, effectively stunning me long enough for him to speak. "I won't help her unless you go upstairs and see to the other woman."

I snarled and briefly considered kicking a man I adored and respected in the balls, but then Jack whispered in my ear. "Go get the answers we need from the woman upstairs. Do it for your sister."

And that did it. For my sister, I went into work mode and climbed the stairs with a fierce determination. Come hell or high water, I would find out who was responsible for this mess, and they were going to pay.

When I reached the kitchen, Matt was standing off to the side keeping his eyes on a woman curled into a ball in the far corner. "Local PD will be arriving any minute now."

"Ma'am, my name is Tatum. If you'd like to avoid the bullshit interrogating, poking, and prodding that the city officers are going to subject you to, I need you to get up and come with me. We'll go out to my car and talk," I said in an even tone. I didn't believe in talking to victims like they were children or on the verge of having a breakdown. Until they'd proven they weren't of sound mind and body, I would speak to them the same as I would any sane adult.

"Okay," she rasped and slowly got to her feet. Her eyes widened when she heard the sirens in the distance.

"Follow me," I instructed and led the way to my SUV. Once she was in the front seat, I backed out of the driveway and parked on the street two blocks from my sister's house.

"Did you know my sister?" I asked.

"Is she the woman wh-who, who w-was—"

"Who was lying on the floor in a pool of blood? Yes, that's my sister."

The woman gasped and started to cry. Then, she shook her head. "No, I didn't know her. The first time I saw her was right before..."

"Right before someone tried to kill her!" I wanted to scream but forced myself to outwardly appear calm. "I need you to tell me what happened in there," I said, hoping it didn't sound like the plea it was.

She turned to face me and met my eyes. After

studying me for several moments, she asked, "Who are you?"

Smart girl. "I'm the person who can help you; I'm also the person who can make you disappear."

1

BATTA

Sweat dripped from my nose and chin as my fists connected with the bag over and over again. I knew I was overdoing it, but I couldn't bring myself to stop. After almost a year together, Kennedy ended our relationship over dinner, and I needed an outlet.

Honestly, I couldn't be upset with her. I'd known for a while things weren't working out between us, but I couldn't bring myself to tell her because I didn't want to lose our friendship. And that's what we were and had been for the majority of our time together—friends.

Kennedy and I had a lot of fun together, but the spark just wasn't there. We'd only slept together twice, and the last time was over six months ago.

So, there I was, the big, scary biker nearing his thirties and single again. Sure, I could go out and pick up some random pussy if I wanted to get laid, but I wanted more than that. I wanted what many of my brothers had recently found—a woman to share my life and build a family with. A good woman.

"What did that bag ever do to you?" Bronze asked from behind me.

I ignored him and continued laying into the bag. My fists were throbbing, and my arms felt like noodles, but I didn't give the first fuck.

"Seriously, man, what's going on?" Bronze asked and stepped up behind the bag.

"Nothing. I'm just blowing off some steam," I said and started stripping off my gloves so I could wipe the sweat from my face.

"Yeah, I can see that. What's got you all steamy?" he asked with a raised brow.

Fuck it. If I didn't tell him, he'd find out sooner or later. "Kennedy and I broke up earlier today. A part of me knew it was coming sooner or later, but it still sucks."

"Damn, man, I thought you two had a good thing going."

I nodded. "We did. We had a good *friendship* going."

"Ah, gotcha. You want to go have a few drinks at the clubhouse?" he asked hopefully.

"I think I'll pass," I said and started to head for the showers. "Oh, if Layla's there, don't mention this to her. I don't want her reactivating my profile on that damn dating site."

Bronze threw his head back and laughed. "You have to admit, that's how you met Kennedy."

"True, but look how that turned out."

"All right, man. I'll keep it to myself. Catch ya later. Oh, be sure to lock up when you leave," he said and headed for the back door.

"Will do." I headed for the locker room after I put my equipment away and wiped my sweat from the bag and the floor. It was after hours, but I had to take a quick shower before I headed home. I couldn't have my bike smelling like my sweaty ass, literally.

I rounded the corner, headed to the shower, and froze in my tracks. About ten feet in front of me, Bronze was on the ground with the handle of a knife sticking out of his chest, gasping for breath. Instinctively, I reached for my gun only to realize I'd locked it in the office when I first arrived. Fuck!

Turning, I quickly glanced around the gym looking for the motherfucker who wasn't going to live much longer. When I didn't see anyone, I started to move toward my brother while my eyes continued to search for the threat. Bronze's gurgling gasp had my attention going straight to him. His lips were moving as he tried to lift his hand.

"Stay with me, brother. I'm going to get you some help," I said quietly. Bronze's eyes widened just as searing pain pierced my back—not once, but twice—and stole the air from my lungs. I tried to turn, to see who was behind me, but I couldn't move. All I could do was close my eyes as I fell face-down to the floor.

2

TATUM

"Are we almost finished?" I asked my sister in the whiniest voice I could muster. We'd been at work for over ten hours and I was beyond ready to go.

"All of this has to be done before the store can open. Might as well do it now while we're on a roll."

"*We* are not on a roll. You might be, but I'm sure as hell not. My roll stopped two hours ago."

She sighed in exasperation. "Fine. Whatever. You can leave, but I'm staying for a few more hours. I want to at least finish the Romantic Suspense section."

"If I leave, how will you get home?"

"I'll drive the truck home," she said simply. "The question is how will you get home?"

Shit. "We drive separately next time," I grumbled causing her to laugh. We didn't have that option; with only one vehicle, we had to ride to the store together. Besides, I couldn't leave her alone, and she knew it.

I briefly contemplated throwing her over my shoulder and carrying her out to the truck, but decided against it, and went to the office to find something productive to do while sitting. I was exhausted from moving boxes of new and used books all day.

Just as my ass hit the soft leather of the office chair, I heard a sound that couldn't be mistaken for anything else. And then I heard it again. Right on cue, Josie came running into the office with wide, fear-filled eyes. "Did you—?" she started.

"Shhh!" I hissed and pulled my gun from the holster at the small of my back. "Go to the safe room and call 9-1-1," I whispered.

"No, Tay! Don't go," she pled, but I was already on my way to the back door.

I pushed it open as two figures dressed in black came out of another door several feet down from ours. And one of those figures had a gun in his hand.

"They're not dead," a male said.

"They fucking will be before anyone gets to them. Now, shut the fuck up and let's get out of here," another male said.

I raised my gun and took aim. "Hey, fuck nuggets, drop your weapon and let me see your hands!"

"You stupid bitch," the one with the gun said as he whirled around and fired his weapon at the same time I fired mine.

As his body was dropping to the ground, I ignored the burning pain in my arm and immediately fired another round hitting the other guy. He grabbed his shoulder and bent forward crying out in pain. "Put your hands where I can see them!" I ordered.

Did he? Of course not. "Hands in the air or I'll wing the other side."

While he held his shaky hands out in front of him, I stepped closer and kicked the gun away from the man on the ground. I was pretty sure he was dead, but I wasn't going to take my eyes off of the other guy to check.

When sirens sounded in the distance, the

dumb fucker spun on his heels and took off running, which thoroughly pissed me off. I couldn't chase after him and leave Josie in danger, and I couldn't bring myself to shoot him from behind, especially when I wasn't sure if he was armed.

"Tay," my sister whispered from the door, clearly not in the safe room where she was supposed to be.

"I'm okay, Jo, but I need to check on the people next door. Pick up the gun on the ground and bring it to me."

While Josie did as I asked, I moved closer and bent down to feel for a pulse. As I suspected, I didn't find one. "He's dead. Let's go see if we can save the others."

I went to the door I'd seen the men come out of and yanked it open. Josie and I gasped at the same time. One man was flat on his back with the handle of a knife sticking out of his chest. Several feet away, another man was face down on the floor with two gunshot wounds to his upper back.

"Go check for a pulse and don't touch that knife! If he's got a pulse, clear the blood from his mouth and help him breathe," I instructed while I ran to the other man who was losing an alarming amount of blood, but was thankfully still breathing.

I pulled my shirt off and covered one bullet hole with it while I scrambled to find something else to press against the other wound. Just as I was about to ask Josie for her shirt, the back door flew open and two police officers stepped inside with guns drawn.

"We're the ones who called! We heard the gunshots. These two need help, right now!" I yelled before either one of them could utter a word.

"Put your hands in the air and move away from the body," one of the officers commanded.

"If I put my hands in the air, he'll bleed to death. The man who did this is outside on the ground. My weapon is tucked into the back of my pants, which you can clearly see. You're welcome to come get it. My sister has the assailant's weapon. Now, please help us!"

Before the officers could even blink in response, the hall was flooded with men approaching from the other side. Big, muscular, leather-clad men. "Where in the fuck is the ambulance?" one bellowed as he landed on his knees beside my sister.

"Let me help you," another one said as he knelt down beside me and pressed a cloth to the unattended gunshot wound.

"Move and let them in!" someone shouted.

"Don't touch that fucking knife!" I yelled. The last thing they needed was some overzealous newbie yanking the knife out and killing the man's chances of surviving.

"He knows what he's doing," the guy beside me said. "He's a friend of ours and a good paramedic."

When two more paramedics arrived beside us, I carefully removed my hands and stepped out of the way so they could take over. As soon as Josie saw me, she came over and stood so close to me I could feel her body trembling.

"Savior, go with Batta. Copper went with Bronze. I'll be there as soon as I can," the man said and turned to face me. "My name's Judge. Thank you, both of you, for helping our friends tonight. Can you tell me what happened?"

"I can, but the cops are going to want to hear it, too, so could we gather the pertinent folks and make this a one-time deal?"

His posture suddenly changed. "You got somewhere more important to be right now?"

"Yes, as a matter of fact I do. I'd like to go have this bullet pulled out of my shoulder before it gets infected and causes my arm to rot off. That would totally fuck up tank tops for me," I snapped.

He stepped back and his eyes went straight to my shoulder. I pulled the wide strap of the tank I was wearing to the side, so he could see the bullet wound. "Fuck! Coal! Get her to the hospital. Now!"

"Calm your tits, bro. I'm good for a little while. I just don't want to be here for hours saying the same damn thing over and over again," I explained.

"Gotcha. Listen, let my friend drive you to the hospital. The cops can get your statement there."

I snorted. "Sorry, Your Honor, I'm sure you're good people and all, but they're going to confiscate my weapon. I'm not going anywhere with a man I don't know without a weapon, especially while I'm injured. My sister can take me, and we can all chat there," I told him and grabbed my sister's hand. "Come on, Jo. I've got a date with a doctor, and I don't want to be late."

3

TATUM

"Do you want me to drive?" I asked Josie as soon as we were in the parking lot.

"Are you crazy? You have a bullet in your arm. I can drive, Tatum," she snapped. "And for the record, I'm not the delicate little flower you seem to think I am."

She was. She just didn't like to admit it, but I kept that to myself. "Okay, I was just checking. I mean, gunshots and stab wounds aren't everyday things for you."

"They aren't everyday things for the majority of the population, but that doesn't mean that the majority can't handle a crisis when faced with one."

"Understood," I conceded and got into the car.

Josie wasn't like me. She was what most people would refer to as normal. Me? I was born tough and had hardened over the years. Things didn't faze me like they did other people. Add to the fact that I was a female—a pretty female—and I was almost always the oddball of any group. And dating? Dating was damn near impossible for me. They didn't make men that could handle me, not without being abusive assholes. Or I should say, without trying to be abusive assholes. Because, well, the two that tried ended up with broken bones. So, as long as I had a fresh set of D batteries, I was perfectly content without a man in my life.

My thoughts were interrupted when Josie pulled into the hospital parking lot. We walked inside to find the waiting room packed with people, many of whom were wearing a combination of leather and denim. "Please fill out this form and have a seat until one of the nurses calls your name," the receptionist said.

In big, block letters, I wrote "I'VE BEEN SHOT" as my reason for being seen and handed it back to her. When she looked up with wide eyes,

I pulled my tank top strap to the side and pointed to my wound.

"Oh! Oh my! Yes, ma'am. Right this way," she stammered and scrambled to push the door open. "Gunshot!!" she screamed, causing everyone in a one-mile radius to focus their attention on me.

I smiled and waved at the staff staring at me. "That's all her. I'm not even bleeding right now."

A woman dressed in scrubs came over to us. "Let's get you in a room and see what's going on."

"I was shot in the shoulder," I said and then shrugged with my good side. "Eh, or maybe it's considered the arm. Either way, it didn't hit anything major; it's just stuck in the meat. I just need someone to pluck it out, clean it, and maybe hit me with some antibiotics."

The woman looked at me like I was insane. "What? It's not the first time I've been shot. If you've got some of those insanely long tweezers, I'll fish it out myself."

"Tay," Josie scolded. "Stop scaring the nurses with the freak show that is you and get on the bed."

"That hurts, Jo. It really does," I snarked, but hoisted my ass onto the bed.

"My name's Kennedy, and I'll be your nurse tonight," she said and sniffled. "Let me take a look at your wound before I grab one of the doctors."

Once again, I pulled my strap to the side. She came closer and inspected the wound for a moment. "Oh, you really aren't bleeding. Okay, let me get one of the doctors. We just had two emergencies come in, so it might be just a few minutes," she said and looked like she was fighting back tears.

"Hey, are you okay?" Josie asked.

She sniffled again and nodded her head. "Uh, yes, I'm fine. I'll be right back."

A few minutes later, a doctor entered the room without knocking. "Hello, I'm Dr. Abernathy. I hear you've been shot, too. Well, let's have a look, shall we?" he asked, though it didn't sound like a question. Actually, he sounded rather irritated or inconvenienced by having to deal with me.

While his bedside manner sucked, he did get the bullet out and bandaged my arm much faster than I'd expected. "I'll go finish with your chart, and the nurse will be in momentarily with your discharge instructions."

I rolled my eyes, but kept my mouth shut. The

nurse wouldn't be in with any discharge papers until the police had been in to speak to me, and based on the earlier events, I assumed one or more of the bikers would be in to see me as well.

As if I'd conjured them up myself, two police officers entered the room with Judge and another man right behind them. I glanced at my wrist like I was wearing a watch. "Right on time, boys."

"Tay," Josie scolded yet again.

"I believe I know everyone except you," I said to the man behind Judge.

"Copper Black, President of the Blackwings MC, and I'm the brother of the man who was stabbed," he said and held out his hand to shake mine.

"Taylin Cr-Crawford," I said and firmly clasped his hand. "How is your brother?"

He shook his head and looked at the floor. "He's alive because of you. Thank you," he said sincerely, and it was clear he was struggling to keep his emotions in check.

"He's in surgery right now," Judge added.

"Well, I hope he pulls through. And the other guy?"

"He's also in surgery," Judge answered.

"Okay, let's get to it," I said and proceeded to

tell them exactly what happened from my perspective.

"May I ask what your background is, ma'am?" one of the officers asked.

I scrunched my forehead and pretended to be confused. "My background?"

"You seem to have some formal training in law enforcement as well as first response."

I chuckled and tried to play it off. "Oh, I don't have any training. I just watch a lot of police shows on television. My sister and I are brand new entrepreneurs. We're opening the bookstore next to the gym," I announced hoping to distract them from my obvious fuck up.

"Be sure to stop by when we're open and pick up some books for your wives or girlfriends," Josie blurted while looking like a deer in headlights.

"Thank you; we just might do that," the officer said. "Well, we'll get out of here so the nurses can finish up with you."

"When can I get my gun back?" I asked before they made it to the door.

"Shouldn't be longer than a few weeks. We'll call you when you can come pick it up."

"Thanks," I replied and waved as the officers left. To my surprise, the two bikers were still standing in my room. And then they closed the door.

Copper whirled around and pinned me with eyes that saw far too much. "Now that they're gone, you can tell me what in the actual fuck is really going on here."

"I'm not sure what you're used to, but I don't take orders from you. I told the police everything there was to tell. I'm sure the they'll be happy to give you a copy of the report if you need a refresher," I said and returned my own knowing stare.

"Bullshit," he scoffed and stepped forward in an almost threatening manner that I decidedly did not like. "Did you bring this shit to my door?"

"Prez," Judge warned.

Copper's hand shot up to hold him off. He jabbed a finger in my direction with each word. "Did. You?"

"Did you bring this shit to my door?" I snapped back. "Sorry, big guy, but I can match you endangered sibling for endangered sibling."

"Sorry, little lady, but your sibling looks unharmed. Mine is far from that right now."

I glanced at my sister who was trying her best not to cry. "Did he just call me 'little lady'? Jo, did you hear that, too, or am I having a stroke right now?"

"Prez," Judge said in a low tone. "You need to leave. Now."

Copper inhaled deeply and, with a scathing look in my direction, he turned on his heel and left.

"I'm sorry about that," Judge said. "He's worried about his brother and his friend, and he's not thinking clearly right now."

Before I could reply, the door opened, and another nurse entered my room. "Jonah, I've been looking all over for you," she said and glanced around the room. "Um, I have an update."

"You can tell us, too. Pretty sure one of us is wearing blood that belongs to whoever that update is about."

The nurse didn't even glance at me. She kept her eyes on Judge, also known as Jonah, and waited for his approval. At his nod, she said, "Batta is in recovery. He's awake and asking for you or Copper."

I watched as some of the tension visibly left Judge's body. "I'll be there in just a minute," he said and kissed her forehead.

When she left the room, he turned back to us.

"Again, I apologize for Copper. We're all extremely grateful for everything you did to help Bronze and Batta. If you'll excuse me, I need to go check on my friend."

"Take care, Judge Jonah," I said with a little wave and hopped off the bed. "Can you send that Kennedy chick in here? I'd like to leave while the night is still young."

He cracked a smile. "Sure thing, Taylin. You two take care. And if you ever need anything, the Blackwings will be happy to help."

4

BATTA

Searing pain pierced my back—not once, but twice—and stole the air from my lungs. I tried to turn, to see who was behind me, but I couldn't move. All I could do was close my eyes as I fell face-down to the floor.

"Go check for a pulse and don't touch that knife! If he's got a pulse, clear the blood from his mouth and help him breathe," someone said before I felt pressure on my back.

I wanted to groan in pain. I wanted to get up and help my brother. I wanted to go after the motherfuckers who tried to kill us. But I couldn't. I was too tired. Maybe if I let go, for just a minute, I could regain some strength.

"Jace Ryder Wild III, it is not your time."

"Mom?" I couldn't see her. I couldn't see anything but a gray haze.

She gently placed her hand on my shoulder. "I love you, Trey. Go make me proud."

"I love you too, Mom. I miss you."

"I'm with you every day," she said, her voice fading at the end.

"You're going to be okay," the other voice promised as something was pressed against my back. "Help is on the way. I'm going to do everything I can to help you, but you have to fight, too. Stay with me, big guy. We've got you. *Just a few more minutes."*

One Week Later

"Trey, are you sure you don't want me to stay at your house for a few days?" Kennedy asked for the umpteenth time.

"I'm sure," I said again. I never stayed at my house, and she knew that, but given the current circumstances, staying at the clubhouse wasn't ideal either. "Judge and River have plenty of room at their house, but I appreciate the offer."

"Trey—" she started, but I stopped her.

"Listen, Kennedy, I know you feel guilty about ending our semi-relationship a few hours before I got shot. Try not to think of it like that. Think of it as us confirming our friendship."

Confusion washed over her face for a split second before she threw her head back and laughed. "Oh, thank you, Trey. I needed that."

I reached out and grabbed her hand. "Seriously, though, nothing has really changed between us."

"I know," she said softly. "But it will change when we start dating other people."

I leaned back and gently patted my chest. "Well, it might be a minute before I get back out there. Got to get this body back in shape after a week of hospital food and no exercise."

"You can shut the hell up right now, Mr. Zero Percent Body Fat," she said while she shook her finger at me.

"Knock, knock. Your chariot has arrived," River said and pushed a wheelchair into the room.

"You know good and well my big ass isn't going to fit in that thing. And I'll be damned if I have to spend another week in here because I was impaled in the ass when that sling on wheels breaks. No, thank you. I'll walk," I told her and got to my feet.

"It's hospital policy—"

I held up my hand to silence her. "Save that shit for the people who follow the rules. Now, one of you take me to see Bronze."

"I thought you were the fun one," River grumbled. "Right this way, Bratta."

"What did you call him?" Judge asked.

"Bratta. Like Brat and Batta. No more talking," she snapped and started walking, hopefully toward Bronze's room.

I knew he was okay; I'd been told by Copper, Judge, and every other brother in the club, but I needed to see it for myself. The last time I saw him, he was on the floor with a knife protruding from his chest. That image had haunted me every time I closed my eyes. My thoughts would then automatically go to my dad. I never blamed him for his actions after my mother's death, but after the incident with Bronze, I had a deeper understanding of why he did what he did. I considered Bronze a member of my family, and I would do the same for him.

"Listen, brother, before you go in there, he's doing a lot better. He's still really pale, and he's having a hard time talking. Just didn't want that to shock you," Judge said quietly.

I didn't give a shit if he was as white as the damn bed sheets because nothing could be worse than what was burned into my brain. Eager to replace my last memory of him, I pushed through the door to find Copper and Layla sitting off to the side while Bronze appeared to be sleeping.

Exhaling in relief, I felt a little bit of the tension leave my body. He was pale, and he looked like shit. But he was breathing, and most importantly, the knife was gone.

"Layla, let me borrow some lipstick," I requested, hoping to distract them from my emotions that were so close to the surface.

"What? Why?" she asked.

"I'll tell you later," I said and flashed her my most charming smile.

"You put lipstick on me, and I will get out of this bed and whoop your ass," Bronze declared with one eye cracked open.

I reached for his hand and clasped it in mine. "Fuck," I breathed and tried to swallow over the lump in my throat. "Good to see you, brother. You scared the shit out of me."

"Scared the fuck out of me, too," he admitted. "Copper, get your rude ass up and let the man sit. He was just shot for fuck's sake."

"Twice," I added and held up two fingers while sticking out my tongue.

Copper pushed a chair behind me and stepped to the side. "I was already up and moving before you said anything, you big pain in the ass."

"You love me, and you know it," Bronze grinned.

"I'm going to step out and get some coffee," Layla said.

"I'll join you," River added.

I chuckled. "They must think we have something to talk about."

Copper cleared his throat. "We do have something to talk about," he said seriously.

"Aw, fuck. Do we have to? I wanted to at least have a day to relax before I had to start worrying about shit."

"Cut the shit, Batta. Two men tried to kill both of you, and they almost fucking did. One of those bastards is dead, but the other one got away. That leaves us with two problems—we don't know who they are, and we don't know what they were doing."

"How the hell do we not know who they are if we know one of them is dead?" I asked.

"No identification on the body. No matches

with missing persons reports, fingerprints, etc. The police department is still working on identifying him, but it's been a week, so I'm not getting my hopes up," Copper explained.

"And you said one got away?"

He nodded and rubbed his chin. "Yeah. We thought he'd turn up at a hospital, but we've had a watch on all the hospitals and urgent care centers in a two-hundred-mile radius with no luck."

"Hold on. What am I missing here?" I asked.

"Go ahead, big brother. Tell him the part about the Blackwings Enforcer being saved by the hot chick next door."

His words triggered a flash of dark hair and whiskey-colored eyes filled with worry. I only caught one glimpse of her face when she leaned down to tell me help was on the way, but I remembered feeling her hands touch my body.

"Stay with me, big guy. We've got you. *Just a few more minutes."*

I'd forgotten about her and how much her words—those words—helped me fight the darkness trying to take me. She appeared out of nowhere, like a guardian angel, and saved us both.

My brothers always gave me strength and

reassurance, but the last time I felt comfort like that was from my mother. Her soothing words and gentle touch always gave me the strength to get through any kind of pain I faced, physical or emotional.

I needed to find her. To thank her. But first, I closed my eyes and tilted my head to the sky to whisper, "Thank you," to my mom, because I knew, without a doubt, she was watching over us that night.

"Batta?" Judge asked pulling me back to the present.

"The woman. Where is she?" I demanded.

"Why do you want to know where she is?" Copper asked.

"So I can thank her for saving my life," I replied incredulously.

"You'll be able to easily find her because she and her sister are opening a bookstore next to the gym," Copper said.

5

TATUM

Two Weeks Later

"I'm going to go pick up some lunch," I called out to my sister. "Need anything else while I'm out?"

"Food, woman! I'm getting hangry."

"Well, move your ass to the safe room so I can get going."

She put down the books in her hand and huffed. "I'm going. Now, hurry up, I'm starving."

"Settle down, psycho sister. I'll be back in a few minutes," I chirped as I closed the door and locked it.

When I turned around, I face-planted into a muscular man's chest causing him to grunt. "Fuck," he groaned and stepped back.

"You!" I yelled in surprise. "Holy monkey balls! What are you doing here? Crap. Are you okay? Here, come inside and sit down," I blabbered like an idiot but managed to get the door open. "It's me, Jo! And we have a visitor."

Josie came running into the front of the store with a look of panic on her face until her eyes landed on the biker. "Oh, shit, Tay. What did you do to him?"

"Why do you automatically assume I did something?"

"Because he's not the first person to be injured by your hard head," Josie deadpanned.

"If you must know, he ran into me."

"Will you stop and bring that chair over here?" she asked though it wasn't a question. I pushed the chair over to him, but he refused to sit down. "Are you okay?"

He rubbed his chest and nodded. "I'm fine. It only hurts for a second if I move too quickly or suddenly tense up, like when someone runs headfirst into my exit wound. Warn a man next time, will ya?"

"You plan on visiting often?" I asked.

He laughed. "We own the gym next door and a bar about fifteen minutes from here. We're bound to run into each other from time to time."

So, the bikers were businessmen. I wasn't expecting that. "I suppose you're right. But, we're not open for business and you're clearly still injured. So, why are you here?" I asked and held up my hand to stop my sister before she even started.

He cleared his throat and shifted his stance. "For starters, I wanted to personally thank you for saving my life."

I crossed my arms over my chest and nodded. "You're welcome. What else?"

His eyes trailed over my body from head to toe and back up. I was used to men making googly eyes at me. I was in shape and I had big boobs; I learned to ignore it many years ago. What I didn't like was not being able to read the look on his face. I couldn't tell if it was surprise, indifference, admiration, or something completely different.

"I want to hear about what happened that night," he stated.

"It's all in the police reports. All you have to do is call and request a copy."

"I want to hear it from you," he clarified and met my eyes with a challenging stare.

I snorted and shook my head. He thought I kept something from the police. He didn't know me, but one thing I wasn't was a liar. Well, unless I was forced to be. "Uh-huh. Well, Mr. Biker Man, I was on my way out to pick up lunch, so you can come back and accuse me of lying to the cops some other time."

He flashed me a wicked smile and stood. "Okay, then. I'll return this to you 'some other time'," he said and pulled my gun from the inside pocket of his leather vest.

"Wait!" I blurted before I could stop myself.

"Yes?" he asked with a triumphant grin.

"Is that my gun?" I asked and tried to sound as naïve as possible, which also made me want to vomit. I hated acting stupid, but I was willing to do it if that's what it took to get my gun back.

"It is," he said and held it out for me to see.

I grabbed the gun with one hand and his arm with the other while I swept his feet out from under him. He went down like a sack of bricks leaving my gun in my hand where it belonged.

Unfortunately, he grabbed my shirt and pulled me down with him. I landed hard against his chest, but he quickly rolled us and had me pinned beneath him.

I blinked up at his handsome face and pressed my hips against whatever part of him was resting between my legs. "I bet you're a beast in bed," I moaned and licked my lips. "Will you choke me?"

His mouth dropped open and he pulled back just enough for me to slide my arms to one side and use my feet and hips to roll him off of me. I quickly sprung to my feet, with my gun still in my hand, and took several steps back.

He pressed his hand to his abdomen and took a minute to catch his breath. For a brief moment, I was worried that I'd actually hurt him. Then, he got to his feet and took two steps toward me with his teeth bared. "What the fuck is wrong with you?" he bellowed.

Ignoring his outburst, I squared my shoulders and didn't back down from his intimidation attempt. "It's time for you to leave."

He glared at me for a few long beats and snorted derisively. "Agreed," he spat and headed for the door. Just before it closed, he turned back and said, "I'll be back, Tatum Cross."

"Josie, go to the safe room, right now," I ordered. "If you haven't heard from me in thirty minutes, make the call."

"Tatum, please don't go," she begged.

"Safe room! Now!" I yelled and ran out to my truck. No way was I letting that motherfucker walk away after calling me Tatum.

I pulled out onto the street and followed him, keeping several cars between us until he turned off onto a stereotypical country road. I kept him in sight but stayed back as far as I could. He turned onto a gravel road that was barely visible, and I followed right behind him. I hit the gas and hauled ass down the driveway so he wouldn't have time to be ready and waiting for me.

He climbed off his bike at the same time I came to a screeching halt and jumped out of the truck. "What do you know?!" I demanded.

"Everything," he smirked.

I swallowed my panic and continued to face him, hoping to appear unrattled by his words. "You know nothing."

"Taylin Crawford born Tatum Kendall Cross, twenty-nine years old, never married, mother and father are deceased, one living sibling. Jo Crawford born Josephine Estella Cross, goes by

Josie, twenty-five years old, recently widowed," he said confidently and crossed his arms over his chest.

Every muscle in my body tensed and my heart skipped a few beats before it started pounding in my chest. I fought to control my breathing and maintain a mask of indifference as I tried to formulate a response.

"What's the matter, pretty girl, cat got your tongue?" he taunted.

He didn't know everything. He knew more than he should, but not everything. I just needed to make him believe he did. Exhaling slowly, I arched one eyebrow and smirked.

"Do you have a point? Besides proving that you know how to Google."

He snorted derisively. "Yeah, I have a point. You can take whatever bullshit you've brought with you and get the fuck out of Devil Springs."

"That's not going to happen. Like I told your friend Copper, I don't take orders from you."

"You know, if you and your sister hadn't almost gotten me and my brother killed, I just might like you." He reached down and blatantly adjusted himself. "Not going to lie, your tight little body and sassy fucking mouth make my dick hard as a rock, but even a piece of prime pussy isn't worth dealing with the kind of shit you've got going on."

I licked my lips and ran my hands over my breasts tightly encased in my fitted T-shirt. "Right back at ya, big guy," I said with a wink and blew him a kiss as I hopped back into my truck. "Too-da-loo," I called out and wiggled my fingers in a girly wave before I hit the gas, kicking up dirt and gravel as I drove away.

"Fuck!" I cursed when my phone rang five minutes later. I'd forgotten to call Josie.

"Tatum, what in the hell is going on?" my boss asked. "I got a call from Josie saying she was in the safe room and you were chasing after someone because you'd been compromised."

"Semi-compromised," I corrected.

"Explain."

"Those bikers you claimed were good guys don't know how to mind their own business," I spat.

He sighed in exasperation. "Tatum, I understand why you want to do this on your own—I really do—but it's time to let them help you."

"I don't—" I started, but he kept going.

"Do you want them to keep digging? Do you want to put your sister in more danger?"

"You know I don't," I seethed.

"Go back to the store with Josie and wait while I make a few phone calls."

"Fine," I gritted out and ended the call. The last thing I wanted to do was make nice with the big, broody biker, but I would do anything for my sister, even if I hated every minute of it.

6

BATTA

When Copper called us in for Church, I knew it had something to do with that damn woman and her sister. It was no coincidence that Bronze and I were attacked right after two damsels in distress appeared in Devil Springs. I was at the gym almost every day prior to getting shot and I'd heard nothing about the space next to the gym being occupied. No way in hell was I going to allow a repeat of my past. Women with secrets showing up in our town was trouble we didn't need or want.

"Got a call from Luke Johnson today. He asked for our help looking after two of his acquaintances—sisters Taylin and Jo Crawford, but two of you already know their real names are

Tatum and Josie Cross." Copper paused and looked at Spazz before focusing his angry eyes on me. "I couldn't refuse his request, since we're the ones who may have put them in jeopardy! What in the fuck were you two hoping to accomplish?" he yelled and slammed his fist on the table.

"I was hoping to find out why in the fuck I took two bullets to my back and your brother took a knife to the chest. And I knew it had something to do with them. We almost fucking died! We both have the right to know why!" I roared right back at him.

Every muscle in his body tensed while he glared at me. "You think I don't know that? You think I don't know that I almost lost my blood brother and a man I consider my blood brother? I fucking know, Trey!" He tilted his head back and swallowed before he pinned me with his fury-filled eyes. "We're helping protect those women. No more searches. Church dismissed."

I shoved away from the table and got to my feet. "Nah. Fuck this. I'm not putting my life on the line for some bitch I don't know. A-fucking-gain," I declared and turned to leave.

"Yes, you will!" Copper shouted. "It's a fucking order!"

I met him stare for stare. I was fucking furious and I didn't give the first shit who knew it.

With a clenched jaw, Copper gritted out, "I don't have to explain myself to you or anyone else, but we all know it's the right thing to do. And we're fucking doing it. Now, get out of my face before you really piss me off."

And fuck if that didn't piss me off even more. President or not, I didn't like being told what to do by anybody. Especially when I knew I was right.

I stormed out of the clubhouse, unsure of where to go or what to do to let off some steam since I hadn't been cleared to return to the gym. Technically, I hadn't been cleared to ride either. "Fuck it," I muttered and climbed on my bike.

Twenty minutes into my ride, a familiar truck pulled onto the road a few car lengths in front of me causing me to smile. We'd see how Little Miss Secrets and Lies liked being followed.

My smile quickly disappeared when I noticed I wasn't the only one following her. "Call Copper," I said and impatiently waited for him to answer.

"Thought it'd take you longer to pull your head out of your ass," he grumbled.

"Someone's following Tatum."

"Fucking hell, Batta—"

"Not now, Prez. If we're supposed to be helping, we gotta let her know before she lets them follow her to the store or wherever she lives."

"Stay behind them and stay on the line." Muffled sounds filled my helmet followed by Copper's voice, though I couldn't make out what he was saying.

"Drop back a few more cars. Dunk and Underwood should be coming up behind you any minute. They're going to pull her over. When they do, you keep going for a while. Then, turn back and come to the clubhouse. Coal's going over to the store to check on the sister."

"What about Tatum and the pricks following her?"

"Tatum is going to be arrested and the truck will be impounded. If they've made the truck, she can't keep using it anyway. Luke will work out the rest of the details," he explained.

"And the prick following her?" I repeated.

Copper cleared his throat. "Luke's handling that."

"Yeah, I'm not feeling any of this shit, Prez," I

grumbled.

"So you've said, and I get it. But, we weren't asked to take over and handle things our way; we were asked to assist."

"See ya in a few," I said and disconnected the call. I couldn't remember ever disagreeing with a decision made by the club, but I was not on board with the decision to blindly help these women. We didn't know the first fucking thing about what we were getting into, and I had a feeling, deep down, that it wasn't something simple like an abusive ex-husband. No, these women were running from something much bigger. Something big enough to involve the FBI. And I'd be damned if I let someone else's secrets and lies take another member of my family away from me.

When I saw the blue lights in my mirror, I kept my eyes on the black Lexus sedan with the tinted windows and the paper tag. Part of me wanted to laugh at how obvious it was. A simple baseball hat and any Honda or Toyota would have been much more inconspicuous.

As expected, the sedan took the next turn after Tatum was pulled over. Then, I did something I never thought I would do; I ignored an order from my President and followed the car.

7

TATUM

Fuck! I was being followed by some cockwad in a black sedan who wasn't even trying to be conspicuous. Oh, and a big ass, grumpy biker.

I thanked the stars above that my phone was synced to the truck and set to accept voice commands. "Hey, Siri, call Luke Johnson."

"Okay, Badass Queen, calling Luke Johnson."

"Johnson," he answered.

"I've got a tail," I said without preamble.

"I'm pulling up your location. Do you recognize them?" he asked.

"No, not the one I'm concerned about. The grumpy biker is also following me."

Luke snorted. "They're all grumpy. Be more specific."

"Big guy. Short beard. Dark blonde hair with a hint of red cut in a short Mohawk. Mischievous blue eyes. I saved his life. Oh, and he goes by Batta." The one I wouldn't mind fucking a time or two.

Luke huffed. "Next time give me the name first if you already kn—" A phone ringing interrupted his words. "Hang on, Tatum. Keep driving."

"Oh, that's a brilliant plan. I hadn't thought of that," I snarked.

Luke didn't take the bait and the line fell silent for several long minutes before he returned. "You're not going to like this, but it was the best I could do. A local cruiser is coming to pull you over. You'll be arrested and the truck will be impounded. You'll be bailed out in a few hours and I'll arrange another vehicle for you."

"What about Josie?" I asked. "She's at the shop by herself."

"I've already sent one of the bikers over to get her."

"Yeah, that doesn't make me feel any better. The one tailing me isn't my biggest fan, and their President is kind of an asshole."

Luke cleared his throat and lowered his voice.

"My nephew, Coal, is a member. That's who I sent to get Josie."

I breathed a sigh of relief upon hearing his words. I'd heard a lot about Luke's sister, Kathleen, and her family since I'd been working with him. So much so, that I felt like I knew them personally. "If I'd known your nephew was in the club from the beginning, I likely would've been a lot more receptive to this plan."

Luke chuckled. "You and I both know that's bullshit. You aren't receptive to anything."

I laughed. "I know. And that's why you love me."

"All right, you little pain in the ass, go get yourself arrested."

"You know how I love handcuffs. Did you ask them to be rough with me?" I joked.

When he snorted a laugh, I could picture him pinching the bridge of his nose and shaking his head while he tried to hide his smile. "Later, Tatum."

Right on cue, flashing blue lights appeared in my rearview mirror. I was tempted to hit the gas and add some fun to this little adventure but figured I shouldn't push my luck and pulled over like a good little civilian.

A female officer got out of the cruiser and approached my truck. "Hello, I'm Officer Dunk. Do you know why I stopped you this afternoon?"

"I do, but the real question is, do you?" I asked and raised one eyebrow.

She laughed. "I spoke with Luke myself. My partner and I are aware of the situation. Go ahead and hand me your license and registration so we can make this look authentic."

"I have a loaded gun under the center console and one in the door," I told her as I reached to get the registration from the glove box.

"Only two? Luke told us you'd have three or four."

"Just two today," I said and handed her the requested items. I only had two because I left one with Josie. I hoped Luke's nephew was able to get her somewhere safe until I could get back to her.

"All right, let's make this look good. I'm going to need you to step out of the car and put your hands behind your back."

"Can you make sure my guns aren't impounded with the truck?" I asked.

She nodded. "My partner is going to grab them, and we'll hang on to them until they magically appear in your new vehicle."

"Thank you." I sighed in relief and climbed out of the truck. "You want me to resist? Shake things up a bit?"

She laughed. "That's up to you, but the more paperwork we have to do, the longer it'll be before you're released. And, unfortunately, there's nothing I can do about the dashcam that's recording all this right now."

"In that case, I'll behave."

FOR A RELATIVELY SMALL TOWN, THEY SURE TOOK their sweet ass time booking, processing, and releasing me from jail. When I was finally allowed to leave, Officer Dunk handed me a large bag with all of my belongings in it. "Your vehicle is parked in the middle row, third space back. Keys are in the bag. Your sister is at the clubhouse," she said and handed me a piece of paper with the address written on it.

"Thanks again," I said and headed for the parking lot. Going to the clubhouse to see the grumpy bikers was not on the list of things I wanted to do after being released from jail.

Actually, it wasn't on any list of things I wanted to do, but Josie was there, so I had to go.

I opened the bag and felt around for the keys while I was walking through the parking lot. My hands wrapped around the familiar metal ring in the bottom of the bag right as I arrived at the third space in the middle row. I looked at the vehicle and then looked around the parking lot for the hidden camera because it had to be a colossal joke. No way in hell was I driving a minivan.

The bag in my hand began to vibrate. Digging my phone out, I wasn't surprised to see Luke's name on the screen. "You have got to be shitting me."

"Sorry, Tatum, it was the best I could do on such short notice. But, it's temporary. From now on, I want you in a different vehicle every few days," Luke explained.

I huffed in annoyance. "Fine, but try to limit the number of minivans I have to drive. I'd prefer a pink Jeep over this, and you know how I feel about pink."

"Were you always this much of a pain in the ass?"

"The survey says yes."

He sighed. "Get in the damn van and go to the clubhouse. Copper is waiting for you."

"If your goal is to get me there, you're going about it all wrong."

"Tatum," Luke growled in the tone that meant he was close to losing his patience with me.

"Fine. I'll go talk to the grumpy bikers," I reluctantly agreed and ended the call.

I cringed as I climbed into the minivan and began to putter down the road. Hopefully, I wouldn't pick up another tail because there was no way I would be outrunning anybody in my new ride. I'm sure there were plenty of people out there who loved them, but I was, and always would be, a truck girl. It didn't matter to me if it was fifty years old or brand new as long as it had a big engine and a nice rumble.

I pulled up to the clubhouse gate and started to roll down my window, but a young man waved me through. I parked where a few other cars were parked—none of which were minivans—and walked up to the closed doors. Was I supposed to knock?

Fuck it. I didn't even think about it. I just yanked the doors open and walked inside. According to Luke, they were expecting me.

"Greetings, grumpy bikers. I'm here to see your leader."

The room fell silent. I glanced around and realized there were no men in the room. "Well, shit, am I in the wrong place? Who cares? If this is a girls only MC, how do I join?"

A beautiful blonde woman laughed and stepped out from behind the bar. "You must be Tay. I'm Layla," she said and extended her hand to me. "Copper's in his office. Follow me."

"Well, damn. I knew it was too good to be true," I said and followed her down the hall.

She knocked on the door as she pushed it open. "Tay's here," she said and stepped to the side so I could enter.

When she started to close the door and leave, I said, "You should stay. I don't really like him."

Layla cleared her throat and gave Copper a pointed look. He sighed and sat back in his chair. "I apologize for being an asshole to you at the hospital," he gritted out.

The amount of effort it took for him to say those words to me made me want to laugh, but I somehow managed to contain it. I could tell he wasn't the kind of man who apologized often. "Uh, thank you for that," I replied with a curt nod. When the room fell silent for several beats, I added, "This awkward moment was brought to you by the letter S."

Copper's lips curved up into a small grin and Layla burst into a fit of laughter. "Oh, I like you. Copper, be nice to my new friend," she said.

"I hear ya, Locks," he replied before she closed the door on her way out.

The moment she was gone, all traces of humor vanished from my face. "Where is Jo?"

Copper held his hands up in a placating manner. "She's in one of the rooms down the hall. She knows what's going on, and she's okay."

"I'd like to see that for myself," I stated firmly. I had no intentions of discussing anything with him until I'd seen Josie, and I told him just that.

"We need to discuss one thing first. We've been made aware of your real names. How do you want to handle that?"

"Who's 'we'?"

"The members of my club; the officers to be exact."

I shrugged. "I have no intentions of being out in public with any of you, so go ahead and use our real names around here."

"Will do," he said and rose to his feet. "Follow

me; I'll take you to your sister." As he led me down a hallway lined with doors, he added, "We already told Riley your names were Tay and Jo, so just go with it so it doesn't confuse her."

Before I could ask who in the hell Riley was, he stopped at the fourth door on the left. He squatted down and knocked the beat of *Jingle Bells* on the wooden door. Just as I was about to question his sanity, a little girl opened the door with a bright smile on her face. "Uncle Mr. President! Did you come to join the tea party?"

Copper scooped the little girl into his arms and tickled her. "Sorry, Princess Riley. I brought a visitor for Lady Jo. This is her friend, Miss Tay."

"Hi, Mistay! Would you like to join our tea party?" she asked excitedly.

I choked on my own spit at the way she pronounced Miss Tay. It sounded like Misty with far too much sass at the end. Seeing Josie in the room trying to stifle a giggle instantly put me at ease. "Hello, Riley. You can call me Tay or Tatum."

"She also likes to be called Queen," Josie added causing me to glare at her. What Siri called me was no one's business but my own.

Riley's forehead wrinkled for a few seconds

before she nodded once. "Okay, you can be a queen, but you can't be my queen." Then, she leaned close to Copper's ear and whispered loud enough for everyone to hear, "Can you put me down now? I need to greet my guest like a proper lady."

Copper chuckled and kissed the top of her head. "As you wish, Princess."

The little girl stood in front of me and curtseyed. "Do come in, Queen Tatum. Would you care for a cup of tea?"

"Yes, please," I said and walked over to have a seat at the card table on the far side of the room.

"Lovely. Please excuse me. I'll be right back with our tea and cookies," she said and left the room with Copper following behind her.

"Are you okay?" I asked Josie the moment Riley and Copper were gone.

"I'm fine. Are you okay? Who was following you?" she rushed out.

"I'm good. I don't know who it was. They didn't try to make a move, and they kept going when I was pulled over. Luke hasn't been able to locate the car anywhere in the surrounding area, so they obviously didn't hang around after I was arrested."

"What're we going to do now?" she whispered. "Are we going to have to go somewhere else?"

"I don't know yet, but we'll figure it out. I'll call Luke back as soon as we get—"

I was interrupted when the door opened, and Riley entered the room with Copper behind her carrying a complete silver tea set. "Well, that's not something I ever expected to see in a biker clubhouse."

"One more word and I'll spill the one with coffee in it," Copper retorted.

I brought my fingers to my lips and pretended to zip them shut. I wanted that coffee. No, I needed it.

Riley climbed into her chair and patiently waited for Copper to pour the drinks. "I'm not allowed to do it because it's hot," she stage-whispered.

Another biker entered the room with a tray full of cupcakes and cookies and placed them on the table. "Thank you, Daddy," she beamed.

"You're welcome, Princess. You have about ten or fifteen minutes to have tea and cookies with your guests before we need to head home," he said and started to ruffle her hair.

"No! You'll mess up my hair!" she shrieked.

"Sorry, Princess," he said and gently tapped the tip of her nose. "Enjoy your party."

I honestly couldn't complain. I hadn't had anything to eat since breakfast and I was starving. With Josie safely by my side, I could spare fifteen minutes to refuel in the company of an adorable little girl.

"So, Princess Riley, tell me your secret. How do you get those growly men to turn into mush?"

Riley giggled and then whispered, "I'll tell you, but you have to pinky promise not to tell anyone."

I held out my pinky. "I promise."

"You have to open your eyes really wide and blink a lot; like this," she said and made the most adorable puppy dog face. "If that doesn't work, then you have to cry a little; but not too much, or your face will get red and icky. You have to be cute." The entire time she was gesturing wildly with her hands and she ended with a curt nod.

It was all I could do to contain my laughter. "Oh, Princess Riley, you have the power to rule the world one day."

"That's what Papa says, too," she said and shoved a cupcake into her mouth.

8

BATTA

I pulled into the clubhouse forecourt several hours later. Despite Copper's order, instinct told me to follow the car, and it was a good thing I did.

"Where in the hell have you been?" Judge hissed as soon as I set foot in the common room.

"Y'all know where I've been. That's why you're here instead of out looking for me," I snapped. I didn't for one second doubt Spazz had tracked my phone. Without another word, Judge turned and walked away from me.

I continued on my way to Copper's office. I knew he was going to be pissed, but I couldn't find it in me to care. Luke wasn't telling us everything we needed to know, and I'd be damned if I let my brothers continue on a path that might get one or more of us seriously injured or killed again.

I rounded the corner to find Copper coming down the hall. His face contorted with rage when his eyes landed on me. "What in the ever-loving fuck is wrong with you? I specifically told you not to follow that car!"

"And you were fucking wrong!" I roared back, barely able to contain my anger.

Judge stepped forward, but not before Copper's fist plowed into my jaw, causing me to rock back on my heels. "I am your President!" he bellowed.

It took every bit of inner strength I had not to react. Had it been anyone else, I would have dodged his punch and returned my own. But, he was my President, and I respected him, even when I was pissed at him.

"There wasn't time to discuss it and put it to a vote. I caught a glimpse of the driver and thought I recognized him. Turns out, I did."

"Who the fuck was it?" Copper demanded.

"One of Luca Peccati's men—Cristofano."

Copper stormed past me and into the common room. "Church!" he yelled much louder than necessary.

Surprisingly, all of the officers were at the clubhouse. As soon as everyone was inside and the door was closed, Copper pounded his fist on the table and ordered, "Batta, tell them what you did today."

Leaning forward and placing my elbows on the table, I gave them the short version. "I noticed a car following Tatum and called it in. To get rid of the tail, Dunk and Underwood pulled her over. I continued following the vehicle. Turns out, it was Luca Peccati's man, Cristofano."

"You sure about that?" Bronze asked.

"One-hundred-percent," I stated. "After Tatum was pulled over, I was about to turn around when he rolled his window down to throw something out and I saw his face. I followed him all the way back to Peccati's estate."

"Damn it!" Copper barked and slammed his fist onto the table. "How in the fuck have we managed to get tangled up with them again?"

I shrugged. "Beats me. Maybe one of the damsels in distress can answer that question."

"Enough, Trey," Copper said quietly, almost calmly, yet there was an edge to it. It was a tone he rarely used, and one that should never be ignored. I took it as the final warning it was and closed my mouth.

"Judge, bring Tatum in here, but make sure Savior or Grant watches over Josie while she's gone."

What in the hell was she doing in our clubhouse? I opened my mouth to ask just that, but Copper anticipated my reaction. "Not a fucking word."

Judge returned moments later with Tatum, who managed to look annoyed while shoving a cupcake covered in pink frosting into her mouth.

"Seriously, Uncle Mr. President, don't you know how rude it is to interrupt teatime?"

When Tatum took her seat, Copper leaned forward and said, "Luca Peccati."

Tatum blinked and replied, "Silver Bugatti?"

"Luca. Peccati."

"Blue. Maserati."

"Oh, for fuck's sake! Does the name Luca Peccati mean anything to you?" Copper yelled in frustration.

"I'd say it's Italian, but other than that, no," she shrugged.

"You've never heard of Luca Peccati or the Peccati family?" Copper asked incredulously.

She shook her head. "No. They must be new, or insignificant, perhaps both. Why do you ask?"

"Because Luca's right-hand man, Cristofano, was the one following you today," Copper blurted.

If I hadn't been watching her closely, I would have missed it; but I saw the slight stiffening of her spine when Cristofano's name was mentioned, and my blood started to boil. This crafty bitch knew more than she was telling us.

"Well, maybe he has a hard-on for me like your boy over there does," she quipped and turned to wink at me. "Yeah, handsome, I saw you back there, too."

"Don't overestimate yourself, sweet cheeks. It had everything to do with watching out for my club and absolutely nothing to do with you."

"Mmkay, Batman. Thanks for clearing that up." With her attention back on Copper, she asked, "Anything else?"

Copper sighed. "Yes, there is, and apparently I'm the one who gets to tell you."

Tatum held up one finger when her phone started to ring. "Sorry, I have to take this," she said and walked out into the hall with the phone pressed to her ear.

"You've got what covered?"

"Are you fucking kidding me?"

"No way!"

"Not happening!"

"I don't care what you think."

"No."

"I said no."

"You know I do."

"There has to be another way."

"Fucking fine."

"Just so you know, I hate you."

"HATE. YOU."

Tatum returned to the room looking like she could spit nails. "Bad news delivered. If you'll kindly point me in the direction of clean sheets and an industrial-size bottle of disinfectant, Josie and I will be out of your hair for the rest of the evening."

"What?" I blurted.

Copper grimaced. "Tatum and Josie will be staying here at the clubhouse with us for a few days. And since you've taken it upon yourself to be more involved than necessary, you'll be playing babysitter. Church dismissed."

9

TATUM

I couldn't believe Luke was making us stay with the bikers. He could have put us in a hotel, in another safe house, or anywhere else that wasn't the clubhouse full of semi-hostile bikers.

I snorted to myself. To be the badasses they were said to be, it sure was easy to get them to blurt out important details by simply pissing them off. Of course, I knew about the Peccati family. Even if they weren't tied to my current case, I'd have to have been living under a rock to not know who they were.

What I did not know was what kind of affiliation they had with the bikers, or why they were questioning me about them.

I returned to the room Josie was in and asked

the current biker babysitter, "Is this the room we'll be staying in for the night?"

"What?" Josie asked.

"I'd have to ask," the young biker mumbled.

"Well, go ask. I'm tired," I snapped.

"What are you talking about?" Josie demanded.

"We're staying here tonight. I'll explain a little later when we have less ears around," I said quietly.

A woman I hadn't met yet knocked on the door as she pushed it open. "Hello, ladies. My name's Leigh. I'm here to show you to your new room."

We dutifully followed her to a room three doors down on the opposite side of the hall. "This is one of our guest rooms. It has a double bed and a pull-out sofa. Both have clean sheets. There's an attached bathroom and there's also a bathroom at the end of the hall. The kitchen is behind the common room. There's plenty of snacks in the cabinets and drinks in the fridge. Help yourself to whatever you like. Do either one of you need anything in particular?"

"Yes, I need a phone charger and neither one of us have clothes or toiletries."

"I'll ask Spazz to bring you a phone charger. My daughter-in-law should be back soon with a change of clothes for both of you. The bathroom is stocked with plenty of toiletries, including new toothbrushes. Anything else?" she asked, not at all offended or intimidated by my bitchiness.

"Damn, you're like the hostess with the mostess, biker style."

"She means thank you," Josie added.

"Knock, knock," Layla called. "I thought you might be hungry, so I brought you some lasagna and garlic bread."

"And I have clothes," another woman announced. I immediately recognized her as one of the nurses from the hospital. So, she was married to Judge Jonah, which meant Leigh was his mother.

"Okay, maybe this won't be so bad," I shrugged and took one of the plates from Layla. I promptly shoved a forkful into my mouth and moaned at the yummy goodness. "Shit. We can't stay here. I'll have fat rolling right out of my pants if this is the kind of food you have. Josie, get your skinny ass over here and eat some of this."

"Filter, Tatum. Use your filter," Josie playfully scolded while the other women laughed.

"It's a biker clubhouse, Josie. I'm pretty sure a filter is not required."

"Only when the kids are here," Leigh added.

I made a show of looking around. "Score! No kids in sight," I said and stuck out my tongue.

The girl who brought the clothes stepped forward and held out her hand. "Hi, I'm River, and I want to be your friend."

I laughed and shook her hand. "That didn't sound creepy at all."

"I thought that was better than 'Hi, I'm River. Would you like to throw knives with me?'"

"Oh, hell yes I would. Let me hoover this lasagna and you're on," I said excitedly.

"Yay!" River squealed and clapped her hands. "No one ever wants to throw with me."

I glanced at the other women in the room. "Really? Why?"

Layla winked. "You'll see."

Josie and I followed the group to the corner of the common room where they had dartboards on the wall behind two pool tables. River took one of the dartboards off the wall and replaced it with a large piece of wood. "Do you want to go first?"

"Nah, you go ahead. Show me what you've got."

She flashed me a grin before she turned and stuck a blade right in the center of the bullseye. Before I could blink, she stuck the second and third blade on either side of the first. "Your turn."

Oh, this was going to be fun. I plucked the blades from the target and returned to where she had been standing when she threw. Then, I took three large steps back and sunk the blades in the same places she did. We continued taking turns, moving farther away from the target each time until we were roughly halfway across the room.

"Do not even think about it!" Copper shouted from behind us. "I don't give a shit if you want to throw over in that corner of the room, but if you want to throw from this distance, you need to do it outside during the day."

"Uncle Mr. President," I whined.

"No," Copper said firmly.

"Fine," I pouted and handed the blades back to River.

"Damn it. I have to work tomorrow and the next day," River grumbled.

"Your next day off will be fine. I don't think we're going anywhere anytime soon," I told her.

"In that case, I'll be back for a rematch in a few days."

With that, Josie and I said our goodbyes and returned to our designated room.

"Before anyone else comes through that door, will you please tell me what in the hell happened today?" Josie asked.

I dropped onto the sofa and exhaled slowly. "When I left the shop to pick up lunch, I noticed I was being followed. Luke called in a favor and had the local PD pull me over and arrest me. The tail disappeared, the truck was impounded, and now we have to stay here for a few days. Oh, and they replaced the truck with a minivan."

"Do you know who was following you?" she asked worriedly.

"I didn't, and neither did Luke, but the big, grumpy biker followed the car following me and figured out who it was."

"Well," she prompted. "Who was it?"

"Cristofano," I whispered.

She gasped and slapped her hand over her mouth as the tears started to slide down her cheeks. "He's trying to find me."

"Looks that way," I agreed.

"Do they know who he is?"

I shook my head. "They know who he is, but not in any way that pertains to us."

"What are we going to do? If he thinks he's found a lead, he won't give up," she said vehemently.

"Luke and I have taken everything into consideration. For right now, we're going to stay here. If we stay out of sight for a few days, he'll think we were just passing through and will start looking somewhere else, especially if we lure him in another direction."

"What if he doesn't?"

"We'll cross that bridge when we come to it. As much as I hate to admit it, these bikers have the means to keep you safe, and I can guarantee no one will look for you here. I know it's hard, but trust me, we'll be okay."

10

TATUM

After our talk, Josie changed into some of the clothes River brought us and fell asleep almost immediately. I, on the other hand, had too much pent-up energy to rest. The longer I stayed in the room and tried to go to sleep, the more I felt like a caged animal. After two hours of tossing and turning, I decided to try something different.

I quietly climbed out of bed, slipped my shoes on, and stepped out into the hallway.

"Where in the hell do you think you're going?" a gruff voice asked, effectively scaring the shit out of me.

"I can't sleep. I was going to walk a few laps around the clubhouse."

"No."

"Excuse me?"

"I said no."

"Noted," I retorted and turned on my heel.

He was on his feet and in front of me in a flash. "You can't go walk laps around the clubhouse, because I'll have to go with you. And I can't watch her if I'm with you."

Well, damn, he sort of had a point. "I pinky promise to be on my best behavior."

"Not fucking happening."

I growled in frustration and came very close to stomping my foot. Taking a step closer, our chests were almost touching when I asked, "Why are you such a pain in the ass?"

"I'm just returning the favor, sugar tits."

I scoffed and turned away from him to go back to my room. Once inside, an idea hit me. I made a beeline for the bathroom and gathered up everything I would need before heading back out into the hallway. "I'm going to take a shower down there, so I don't wake Josie up."

"Those bathrooms don't have showers," he informed me with a cocky grin. I wanted to scream in anger, cry in frustration, and punch him in his smug face. Clearly, I didn't do a good job of hiding those emotions as moments later he sighed and opened the door opposite from ours. "You can take a shower in there."

I cautiously peered inside like I was looking into a portal to Hell. "What's in there?"

"That's my room. You can use my shower." When I hesitated, he added, "Shit or get off the pot, woman."

"If you even think about fucking with me, I will repay the favor in ways you can't even imagine," I warned.

He pinched the bridge of his nose and slowly exhaled. "I'm tired. Go shower so I can go to sleep."

I started to ask how he was going to babysit us while he was sleeping, but thought better of it and kept my mouth shut. I don't know what I was expecting his bathroom to be like, but it certainly wasn't the meticulously clean room I walked into.

I turned the faucet on and then started to casually snoop while the water was heating up. Peeking into the cabinet beneath the sink, I almost fell on my ass when my eyes landed on a box of adult diapers. I couldn't resist. Pulling one from the box, I went back to the hall and held it up in front of Batta's face. "Are you the baby or the daddy?"

He snatched it from my hand and rose to his feet. "I can assure you, sugar tits, I'm the one that does the spanking. Now, mind your fucking business and get in the shower before I take back my kind offer."

I grinned and turned to go back to the bathroom. "Whatever you say, Baby Batta," I called over my shoulder just before I closed and locked the door. He growled in frustration but made no attempt to open the door.

I took my time in the shower letting the hot water wash away my shitty day and ease my sore muscles. By the time the water ran cold, I was ready to crawl into the nearest bed and fall asleep.

When I entered the room, my biker babysitter was sitting on the end of his bed seemingly waiting for me. "Thanks for letting me use your shower," I said and headed for the door.

He snagged the waistband of my yoga pants. "Not so fast. You're sleeping in here."

"Not happening. I need to be with my sister."

"Your sister is fine. She's asleep and her door is locked. I trust she's not going anywhere. You, on the other hand, will probably try to sneak out the first chance you get, and I need to sleep. So, unless you want me to restrain you while I sleep, you'll climb your ass in my bed and lay down."

I RUSHED DOWN THE STAIRS AND STOPPED DEAD IN my tracks. My sister and her husband were lying motionless on the floor as a pool of blood formed around them. Sheldon's injury was obvious, but I couldn't immediately see where Josie was hurt.

"Nooooooo!" I screamed. "No! Oh, please, no! Josie! I need help! Fuck! Somebody help me!" I wailed while I frantically tried to search my sister's body for a wound.

Large hands landed on my shoulders and tried to pull me away. "Let me help her," Dave said softly. "Go upstairs, Tatum. You don't need to see this."

"I'm not leaving her," I cried.

"That girl up there needs a woman to help her. Go!"

I twisted and shoved him away as hard as I could. "I'm not leaving her," I cried and didn't bother to wipe away the tears clouding my vision.

"I'm not leaving her! I'm not leaving her! I'm not leaving her!"

I startled awake when someone shouted, "Tatum!" My eyes popped open, and I tried to sit up, but my wrists were held tightly in someone's grasp. I tried to pull away, but he wouldn't let go. "You were having a nightmare, and beating the shit out of me," he said and slowly released his grip.

I rubbed a hand over my face and quickly took in my surroundings. "Fucking hell. I was hoping the part about me being in your bed was part of the nightmare."

He sighed in exasperation. "It wasn't. Now be quiet and go back to sleep."

As much as I wanted to argue with him, I was exhausted, warm, and comfortable. There was no way I was getting out of his bed just to prove a point. Instead, I settled for rolling over on my side.

His big arm wrapped around my waist and pulled me back against his chest. In some sort of practiced man maneuver, he turned me back to face him and wrapped his other arm around me. "Just go to sleep. I promise I won't tell anyone Queen Badass likes to snuggle."

I did like to snuggle, and much to my chagrin, I was thoroughly enjoying snuggling his warm, muscular chest. Before long, my eyes closed and I may or may not have mumbled, "You smell good," before I fell asleep.

THE NEXT TIME I WOKE, I WAS ON THE SOFA IN the room with Josie. "What the?" I muttered to myself. Had it all been a dream?

"Batta brought you in here a few hours ago," she snickered. "He didn't know I was awake, but I saw him gently place you on the sofa and cover you with a blanket. He even smoothed your hair away from your face."

I held my hand out. "Stop talking."

"You know, you could try being nice to him," she suggested.

"I was nice to him. He's the one who started this."

"Was he? Are you sure about that?"

"I'm pretty sure. It doesn't really matter, anyway."

"If it doesn't matter, try being nice. Momma always said you could catch more flies with honey than vinegar."

"I'm not trying to catch him, Josie."

She sighed. "You know what I mean. Being

friendly might make our stay here a little more pleasant." She paused and cocked her head to the side. "Unless you're enjoying this weird, angry sexual tension the two of you have going on."

I scoffed. "Well played, Josie."

Fucking great. One more thing to add to the list of shit I did not want to do. Being nice to the asshole biker was up near the top with driving a minivan.

11

BATTA

I sat at a table in the corner of the common room and watched as Tatum and Josie quietly ate breakfast. They didn't look anything alike. Tatum was average height with an athletic build. She had dark, brown hair and amber eyes — similar to the color of whiskey or warm honey. Josie was the polar opposite with light blonde hair, pale skin, and light-colored eyes. She was also several inches shorter than Tatum and was potentially underweight. Maybe they had different fathers, or perhaps different mothers. Maybe they were adopted.

I shook my head and laughed to myself. What in the hell was I doing? It didn't matter what they looked like or what their blood relation was. My only concern was to make sure they stayed at the clubhouse and stayed out of trouble. I didn't need any of their personal details to do that.

Tatum walked over to my table and shoved her hands into her pockets. "So, what's there to do around this place? I'm not used to having a lot of idle time."

"You can throw darts or play pool. I'm sure there're some DVDs around here somewhere. One of the Old Ladies probably has some books around here, too. That's about it," I said and watched her face crumble.

"It's going to be a hell of a long day," she sighed and walked back over to Josie. "We'll be in our cell, I mean bedroom."

It wasn't like it was going to be a walk in the park for me either. They couldn't leave the clubhouse, which meant I couldn't leave. It sucked, but it was what it was.

"Mind if I join you?" Leigh asked as she pulled out a chair and sat down.

"What if I'd said I did mind?"

"It would've been the wrong answer," she replied and took a sip of her coffee. Clearing her throat, she clasped her hands in front of her and met my eyes. "Talk to me, Trey."

I foolishly attempted to act like I didn't know what she meant. "Talk to you about what?"

She arched one eyebrow and stared at me with the "Mom face." I only lasted a minute, maybe two, under her scrutiny before I caved.

"I don't know what my problem is," I admitted quietly.

She reached across the table and placed her hand over mine. "Come with me."

"I can't leave the clubhouse, because I have to keep an eye on Tatum and Josie."

She picked up her phone and started typing what I assumed was a text message to someone. After a few exchanges, she said, "Copper's going to have Coal and Grant watch over the girls until we get back."

Reluctantly, I got to my feet. I had a feeling I knew where we were going.

When we arrived at the cemetery, I assumed Leigh would go talk to her late husband, Jonas, while I went to visit my mother. We'd been to the cemetery together several times over the years, and that's how we'd always done it. However, Leigh walked over to the bench near Mom's grave and took a seat. She looked at me expectantly and patted the bench.

When I sat down beside her, she reached over and took my hand in hers. "Your mother was one of my best friends. Not a day goes by that I don't think about her. Years ago, maybe when you were five or so, she made me promise to be a mother to you if anything ever happened to her. Hell, me, Goldie, and your mom all promised to be there for each other's kids. Now, I've always loved you like you were my own son, you know that, but I've never felt the need to step in like a mother would, until now. Whatever it is, tell me, and I'll do everything I can to help you."

I pulled my hand from hers and wrapped my arm around her shoulders. Exhaling slowly, I tried to put my feelings into words. "The day I was shot, and Bronze was stabbed, I was at the gym throwing punches at a bag because Kennedy had ended our relationship earlier that day. I'm not upset about that. We'd been friends masquerading as a couple for months. But, I wasn't happy about having to find someone new and start over from scratch. That takes time, and it's even harder for a man like me. I thought I would've been married with a couple of kids by now. I was so caught up having a pity party for myself that I didn't realize someone was in the gym until it was too late."

Leigh turned to me and pulled me in for a fierce hug. "Oh, Trey, you feel guilty," she said as realization dawned. "You have nothing to feel guilty about. I hate to say it, but you getting shot is what saved the both of you. Tatum heard the gunshots and came running."

"I've never been so scared, Leigh. The last thing I remember seeing was Bronze gasping for breath as he choked on the blood coming out of his mouth. And all I could think was, 'We're too young to die. I want more from this life.'"

"You didn't die. You both survived, and you both have a chance to fulfill your dreams."

"I can't move forward with anything until I know who was responsible for trying to kill us and why. And now we have two women who are involved in a world of shit we have to help protect. We have no idea what kind of danger they could be bringing to our door." I swallowed thickly and whispered, "It's just like what happened with Mom."

Leigh sat back and gave me a stern look. "It's not the same," she stated and paused for a moment. "Did it occur to you that maybe your path crossed with theirs for a reason?"

"What reason would that be?"

Leigh grinned knowingly. "Tatum is your game changer."

I shook my head. "No way. She dislikes me just as much, if not more, than I dislike her."

She threw her head back and laughed. "Oh, that's the biggest load of bullshit I've ever heard." She paused and continued to laugh. "Tell me something, Trey. Do you find her attractive?"

"You've seen her. What man wouldn't find her attractive?"

"I'm sure a lot of men would be drawn to her physical beauty, but Tatum is a strong, independent woman. She can take care of herself and doesn't need a man to protect her. A lot of men can't handle that. You, on the other hand, were raised around strong women. And, to be perfectly honest, I think Tatum is just the kind of woman you need."

"Can I ask you something?"

"Of course," she replied immediately.

"You been drinking this morning?"

She laughed and playfully slapped my chest. "Oh, stop. I just want you to be happy. And, grandbabies. I want some damn grandbabies."

"You'll have to talk to Judge and River about that," I told her.

"Oh, I have, but I want grandbabies from you, Copper, and Bronze, too. Consider this my formal request."

I laughed. "Noted."

"Good. Now go visit with your mother so we can get back to the clubhouse, and you can make nice with Tatum and Josie."

I didn't want to "make nice" with Tatum. The more I thought about it, the less appealing it was. The woman was under my skin in a way no one had ever been. She was hot as hell, and she'd even made me laugh a time or two, but she was dangerous in a way that wasn't welcome. One way or another, she had to go.

12

TATUM

We'd been holed up in our little room for several hours after breakfast when I'd had enough. I pulled out my phone and called Luke. "Listen, man, if you want us to stay here with the bikers, we're going to need some stuff from the house."

"Like what?" he asked, sounding annoyed with my very simple request.

"Like clothes, shoes, my laptop, tampons, my glitter nail polish, my bikini wax kit, my—"

"Stop talking."

"Oh, and Mr. Piggles!" I exclaimed.

"Who is Mr. Piggles?"

"He's the stuffed pig I've slept with since Santa gave him to me for my very first Christmas.

I barely slept a wink last night without the familiar comfort of him in my arms," I exaggerated. I did have a stuffed pig that traveled with me everywhere I went, but I'd stopped sleeping with him years ago.

"Damn it, Tatum," he cursed, but I remained silent and waited for him to cave. It didn't take long. "Fine, make a list of the shit you need, and I'll get someone to go over and get your stuff."

"Oh, thank you, my dear friend. You're the best," I chirped.

"Fuck off, brat."

"Speaking of fucking off, Josie, add vibrator and extra batteries to the list."

"Fucking hell," Luke grumbled and disconnected the call.

"Why do you irritate him like that?" Josie giggled.

"Why not? I have to have some form of entertainment while we're stuck here. Otherwise, I'll get myself into trouble." I had always been good at adapting to different situations and finding ways to make the best of it. If making people uncomfortable was a part of it, that was their problem, not mine.

After making a list of the things we needed,

and several items we didn't need, Josie went to take a shower while I tried to find something on television to watch. I'd just selected a movie called *Teeth* about a teenage girl with vaginal dentata when a blood-curdling scream came from the bathroom. I burst through the door with my gun drawn to find Josie standing on top of the toilet frantically pointing at the bathtub.

I turned with my gun aimed and ready to take out the threat, but nothing was there. "What the hell, Josie? I thought someone was trying to kill you," I fumed as I holstered my gun.

"D-d-down th-there," she pointed shakily.

I looked down to see a snake chilling in the bathtub. Sighing, I reached down to pick it up. "It's okay. This is a harmless ball python. I'm guessing it probably belongs to one of the bikers."

"It does," Batta said from behind me. I'd caught a glimpse of him coming into the room when Josie screamed, but hadn't acknowledged him. "They both have a history of being escape artists."

"There's another one?" Josie almost shrieked.

"Yes, there's two. Slither and Squeeze belong to Copper and Bronze."

"Where is the other one?" Josie whispered.

Batta shrugged. "Not sure. They have a couple of favorite hiding places around here."

"I'm going to lock the door and stay in here until the other one is found," Josie declared.

"I'll help them look for it and let you know when it's safe to come out," I assured her.

I heard the lock click when Josie closed the door, but I didn't hear the water start. She was probably too freaked out to even consider getting in the shower.

"You're not scared of snakes?" Batta asked, sounding surprised.

"Why would I be scared of something that can't hurt me? This one is harmless, and I stay away from the ones that aren't," I explained.

"You're probably the first woman in years who's not been afraid of Slither and Squeeze. Most have the reaction Josie did."

"I thought you would've already figured out that I'm not like most women. Now, let's go find this one's friend so my sister can come out of the bathroom. Where should we look?"

Batta grimaced. "Honestly, they usually don't stray too far from each other when they get out.

Slither's probably in here somewhere—under the bed, under the couch, under the covers."

"I don't care where we find it; we're telling Josie it was somewhere not in here," I whisper-yelled.

"Understood."

"What in the hell are you watching?"

I looked up to see the main character in stirrups at the gynecologist's office. "It's called *Teeth*. That girl has a man-eating vagina." On the screen, the doctor screamed and held up his arm, which was nothing but a bloody stump. "See. She bit him."

The look of horror on his face was hysterical. "Who in the hell came up with something like that?"

I doubled over laughing. "It's based on an old wives' Tale women used to tell to discourage their sons, or husbands, from having sex with unknown women. It was also used to discourage rape."

"You mind pausing that while we find the snake?"

"That's what she said." After laughing my ass off and pausing the movie, I draped Squeeze around my neck and proceeded to systematically search the room with Batta. It took us almost twenty minutes, but we finally found Slither curled up behind the DVDs on a shelf below the television. I didn't announce my discovery because I didn't want Josie to hear it, so I quietly scooped the snake into my hands. Immediately, he started to wind himself around my arm. Turning, I held my arm out and whispered. "Found him."

Batta was on the floor looking under the bed, again. He sat back on his heels and looked me over from head to toe. He licked his lips once but continued to stare at me. "What?" I finally asked.

"You look fucking hot with two pythons wrapped around you," he said and palmed his crotch.

I smirked. "Guns, knives, snakes, and tits. Is that what does it for you, big guy?"

He shook his head and got to his feet. "I'll take them back to their cage," he said and extended his hands for the snakes.

"I want to see where they live."

"They live in Bronze's room. Fair warning, I have no idea who's in there or what might be going on."

I shrugged. "Wouldn't be the first time I've walked in on an orgy."

"What?" he asked in surprise.

"You heard me."

"Okay, then. Follow me."

I was slightly disappointed when we arrived at Bronze's empty room. After the situation with the snakes, I was hoping for a little more excitement.

Deflated, I placed the snakes in their enclosure and made sure the lid was latched. After glancing around the room, I noted, "If he'd add some weather stripping to the bottom of the door and keep it closed, the snakes wouldn't be able to escape from his room if they got out of their cage again."

Batta blinked at me with a look of surprise on his face. "That's actually a good idea."

"Why do you seem surprised by it?" I asked, hoping he didn't say something stupid that would get him kicked in the balls.

"I'm surprised none of us thought of it before. They've had those snakes for over twenty years," he explained.

"Oh, well in that case, make sure you tell them it was my idea," I said gleefully.

"Will do," he said with a wink.

I studied him briefly. He was acting like a different person. The grumpy, broody, biker I was familiar with had been replaced with a man who was borderline tolerable. And that made me suspicious. Why did his blatant disdain for Josie and me suddenly disappear?

My stomach growled, giving me the perfect excuse to break away from him. "Gotta go. Audrey has spoken, and she gets really upset if I don't feed her," I announced and rubbed my stomach.

His mouth dropped open and the color drained from his face. "You're pregnant?"

"No, you big oaf! I was talking about my stomach. Haven't you ever seen *Little Shop of Horrors*?"

"I don't think so."

"Good stuff. You should watch it some time," I said and headed back to our room to free Josie from her self-imposed porcelain prison.

A few hours after lunch, I was well on my way to pulling my hair out. The list we made was still in our room waiting for someone to come get it. Apparently, the bikers had day jobs, which meant we weren't going to get our stuff until later in the evening.

I stood from the couch and started to stretch.

Josie looked up from her book. "What are you doing?"

"Getting ready to work out because if I don't do something, I'm going to go crazy. How are you handling this so well?" I asked.

Josie gave me a sad smile. "I've been in worse situations."

Me and my big, unfiltered mouth. It was a blessing and a curse. "I'm sorry. That was incredibly insensitive of me. You must think I'm acting like a spoiled brat."

She started to shake her head and then laughed. "Okay, maybe a little." She held up the book she'd had her face buried in for most of the day—*Betting on Forever* by Scarlett Black. "This has helped tremendously. I love a good book. You should give it a try when I'm finished."

"I only read books that have hot sex in them," I blurted.

"Trust me. You won't be disappointed with this one. And it's about bikers," she said excitedly.

I went back to my improvised workout while Josie continued reading her book. Exercise was doubly beneficial for me; it helped me stay in shape, which was required for my job. It also helped clear my mind, which allowed my critical thinking skills to do some of their best work. I'd had numerous strokes of genius come to me in the middle of an intense workout. And I needed one sooner rather than later.

13

BATTA

After talking to Judge and getting access to the security feed for the clubhouse, I had Spazz pull it up on one of the televisions in the common room so I could watch the girls without having to sit in the hallway all day. I hated being on babysitting duty, and I knew that was part of why Copper gave it to me. Honestly, by most club's standards, I deserved a much harsher punishment for going against a direct order from the President—even though I did have a good reason.

Finally, the typical workday was over, and people started to trickle into the clubhouse. Even Copper, who was usually in his office, had been out all day. He walked in with Judge at his side and came straight over to where I was sitting.

Copper glanced at the TV with the security feed and rubbed his chin. "I like that. I think we'll keep the feed on it from now on."

"Does that mean I'm off babysitting duty?" I asked hopefully.

He laughed. "I don't think so. But, I do need you and one of the boys to go over to Tatum's place and pick up a few things. They have a list of what they need in their room."

"Now?" I asked.

"Might as well do it now while Judge and I are here and can keep an eye on them. Grant's out back. Take my truck and take him with you," Copper said.

"Where do they live?"

"Beats the fuck out of me. You'll have to ask them."

I went down to their room and knocked on the door. Tatum yanked it open, out of breath and covered in sweat.

"What the fuck's wrong with you?"

"Oh, you've probably never seen it before. This is the face of a woman who's just had a magnificent orgasm." Caught off guard by her response, I wordlessly gaped at her. She rolled her eyes. "I was working out, so I didn't die of boredom. What do you want?"

I furrowed my brows. The woman was maddening. "I need your address and the list of shit you want from your place."

"Halle-freaking-lujah! It's about damn time!" she shouted and turned around to pick up a piece of paper from the nightstand. She grabbed a pen and scribbled something on it before handing it to me. "Oh, you'll need a key. One second." She removed a key from her key ring and handed it to me. "My number's at the top. Call me if there's something you can't find," she said and closed the door in my face.

I narrowed my eyes and glared at the door for a few seconds before I went outside to get Grant. He was young, but he was a good prospect. He always did what was asked of him and never complained. He was quiet, more so than the rest of us, but that would probably change over time.

We climbed into one of the club's SUVs and followed the GPS directions to a gated community on the wealthier side of town. "Here's the gate code," Grant said and handed me the list. Once through the gate, we continued on to a large, brick house toward the back of the neighborhood. "The directions say to pull around back and enter through the red door."

I parked behind the house and looked around for where we were supposed to go. "Do you see a red door? Because I sure as hell don't," I asked and turned to Grant who was standing behind me. That's when my eyes landed on a detached garage with a door painted blood red. "There it is," I pointed out.

"Why wouldn't she just tell us they lived behind the house?" Grant asked.

"I want to say it's because she was using code words since they're in a precarious situation, but more than likely, it's because she gets a kick out of being a pain in the ass."

Grant laughed. "Yeah, I can see that."

I unlocked the door and cautiously pushed it open. I wouldn't put it past Tatum to have the place rigged with some crazy ass booby trap she conveniently forgot to mention. When nothing happened, I reached my hand inside, flipped the light on, and waited again. After a full minute, I stepped inside and took my first look at the items on the list.

"You have got to be fucking kidding me. Did you see what she put on here?"

Grant laughed. "I stopped reading when I got to ten pairs of cooter covers."

I pinched the bridge of my nose. No wonder she told me to call if I couldn't find something. Almost everything on the list had some sort of Tatum-ized name.

Pearly Whites Polisher.

Claw Clippers.

Tress Tamer.

Cooter Covers.

Peacock Paint.

Cotton Ponies.

Tit Slings.

The Sphynx Maker.

Tootsie Toasters.

Shit Kickers.

"Fuck it. Find what you can. I'm not wasting time trying to figure out what The Sphynx Maker is."

I found two duffle bags in a closet and handed one to Grant. "You take one bedroom and I'll take the other. Fill that with clothes and a couple pairs of shoes. And whatever else you think they might want."

Of course, I ended up in Tatum's bedroom. As I was stuffing clothes into the bag, I realized Tatum didn't have a wide variety of clothing. Her wardrobe mainly consisted of tactical pants, tank tops, T-shirts, and hoodies. No dresses or dressy clothes anywhere. It made sense. Tatum didn't strike me as a girly girl.

Or so I thought until I pulled open her underwear drawer. I stared down at the array of sexy, skimpy panties paired with matching bras perfectly displayed as if they were in a lingerie store. Before I could stop myself, I picked up a black, lacy thong and pictured her wearing it for me with nothing but her combat boots on as I rubbed the silk between my fingers. With my cock rock hard and ready to go, I shoved the entire contents of the drawer into the bag, including the vibrator stashed in the back, though I removed the batteries first.

"I'm finished. Do you need help?" Grant called from the bedroom door.

"No," I blurted. No way in hell did I want Grant in Tatum's room going through her personal things. And then I realized that's exactly how it sounded. "I'm good in here. Can you look for the laptop, phone chargers, and Kindle?" I blurted, hoping he didn't notice.

"Fuck," I whispered to myself. What in the hell was she doing to me? I wanted to fuck her and strangle her at the same time.

While Grant went in search of the items I requested, I braced myself and entered Tatum's bathroom. I did my best to figure out what she wanted, because there was no way in hell I was coming back for round two. I was digging through the cabinet for cotton ponies—which I assumed were tampons—when my eyes landed on a box with a hairless cat on the front—Brazilian bikini wax kit. The Sphynx Maker. Holy shit. Grabbing it and the box of tampons, I tossed them into the duffle bag and left, because I was fucking done.

As we were leaving, Grant asked, "Who do you think lives in the main house?"

"My best guess is no one. It's probably a safe house owned by the government under a fictitious name."

"If that's the case, why are they living in the converted garage?"

"If you were trying to find them, where's the first place you'd look? The house or the garage?" I asked.

"Ah, I get it. An extra layer of protection," he mused.

"Exactly."

Halfway back to the clubhouse, I noticed a car following me, though it wasn't the same one that was following Tatum the day before. "Keep your eyes on the silver sedan behind us and call Copper. Put it on speaker."

"Copper Black," he answered even though he knew damn well who was calling.

"Got a tail, Prez."

"Son of a bitch!" he roared. "Where are you?"

"Coming through town about to hit Main Street."

"Do you know who it is?"

"Not a clue. It's not the same car that was following Tatum yesterday," I relayed.

"Act like you haven't noticed them and come back to the clubhouse. Serious as fuck, Batta, if I don't see you pulling up to the gate in less than fifteen minutes, I'll have your ass and probably your patch," he growled.

"Understood, Prez. We're on our way." I waited until the call ended and cursed. "Damn it!

I wanted to fuck with him a little bit before we got there."

Grant grinned. "Now that would've been fun."

"It's always the quiet ones," I laughed.

Between the two of us, we kept our eyes on the car. He stayed a couple car lengths back and followed us all the way to the clubhouse. I was surprised to see the gate open and every brother standing in the forecourt with their arms crossed over their chests. I could barely see the barrel of a gun peeking out from under Copper's bicep when I passed by to park behind them.

Just as Grant and I got out and moved to stand with the club, the car approached at a snail's pace and almost came to a complete stop in front of the open gate. From that point, everything happened in slow motion.

The driver of the car cracked the window.

The barrel of a gun appeared.

Every one of the brothers, including myself, took aim at the car.

A horn blew, and tires squealed.

An eighteen-wheeler slammed into the back of the car, effectively destroying the vehicle and everything in it.

"Holy shit," I breathed.

Splint took off running to the semi-trailer.

"Judge, go make sure we're not visible on the security feed. Grant, call 9-1-1," Copper barked and headed toward the wreckage.

"Where are the girls?" I asked.

"Inside with Bronze. Go let Tatum know what's going on and make sure she stays inside."

I grabbed the duffle bags from the SUV and took them inside just as sirens sounded in the distance.

Tatum was already making her way down the hall with a gun in her hand. "What in the hell was that?" she demanded when her eyes landed on me.

"Car accident right in front of the clubhouse," I said casually. I held up the duffle bags and smiled. "Here's your stuff."

She holstered her weapon and eyed me warily. "Uh, thanks," she replied and took the bags from me. "I'll just put these down in our room and see if they need any help outside."

"No, you won't. Copper specifically said for you to stay inside."

She arched an eyebrow. "Oh, really? And why did he specifically say that?"

I exhaled slowly. "Because we picked up a tail on the way back from your place. It stopped in front of the clubhouse and was probably going to start shooting, but a tractor-trailer plowed into the back of it before they could get a shot off."

"Is the driver of the car dead?" she asked in the way one would ask if it was raining.

"That hasn't been confirmed, but I'm almost one-hundred-percent certain the answer is yes." There was no way anyone in the car survived. Hell, the majority of the car didn't survive.

"Okie dokie. Thank you," she said and disappeared into her room.

14

TATUM

Josie was curled into a ball on the bed and shaking like a leaf. Dropping the bags on the end of the bed, I pulled her into my arms. "It's okay. There was a car accident on the road in front of the clubhouse. We're not in any danger," I soothed.

"Are you sure?" she asked through her tears.

"I'm positive. There's absolutely nothing to be worried about."

She sat up and wiped her nose with her hand. "I'm so ready for this to be over," she whispered.

"I know you are. And, so am I. But stuff like this takes time, and trust me, we don't want to rush it."

"I know. I just…I'm tired of being scared all the time. And I want to go home," she sniffled.

"That's the end goal, sweetie. To make it safe for you to return home."

"That's never going to happen," she whispered. "No matter what happens, the home I knew and loved is gone, and I won't ever be able to get it back."

I cocked my head to the side. She'd never said anything like that before. "What do you mean?"

"I'm in this mess because of him. It doesn't matter how much I loved him or how much he loved me; I'm not going to fight my way out of this mess only to go right back into the situation that caused it in the first place."

"Do you really think he's responsible for what happened to you?" I asked. If he was, we needed to refocus our investigation.

She shook her head. "Do I think he's directly responsible? No. I don't think he had anything to do with it. But indirectly? Yes. I was put on their radar because of who he is."

"Are you sure about that? I mean, did you hear or see something that led you to believe it was because of him?" I asked, excited to be getting some new information.

"Yes and no," she said hesitantly. "I remember hearing Sheldon say that I was extra special because I served two purposes—revenge and money. Then he laughed about what his face would look like when he found out what happened to me." She inhaled deeply and straightened her shoulders. "I just want you to know that your efforts won't be wasted. I won't squander the second chance I was given the day you came running because your sister needed help."

I took a moment to carefully choose my words. "As long as you're happy, it will have been worth it. Don't make decisions based on what you think I would or wouldn't approve of. Because at the end of the day, this isn't about me."

"You're a good person, Tatum."

"Yeah, well, I'm sure there's quite a few who would disagree with you," I said uncomfortably. I never knew what to say when someone complimented me.

She grinned knowingly. "Are you referring to our biker babysitter?"

I narrowed my eyes. I knew that tone. "Actually, I wasn't, but I don't like what you're insinuating."

"Oh, come on. The sexual tension between the two of you is so hot even I get a little wet when you're both in the same room."

My eyes widened in complete and utter surprise. "What?" I asked, my voice coming out an octave higher than usual. "There is absolutely no sexual tension. None whatsoever!" Yes, I would fuck him wearing a bell around my neck hoping the cows would come home, but anything more than that was a hard no from me.

I whirled around when the door opened behind me. Batta stood there with a shit-eating grin on his face. "I knew you wanted my dick. But let me hear you deny it some more."

"There's a big difference between wanting *your* dick and wanting *a* dick," I said evenly while I planted my palms on his chest and shoved him out the door.

Unfortunately, he grabbed on to my wrists and pulled me along with him. Pivoting, he put my back against the opposite wall and raised my hands above my head. Dropping his head, he ran the tip of his nose along my jaw and inhaled deeply. "You need to be fucked, sugar tits?"

Yes. Yes, I did. But no way in hell was I admitting that to him. Instead, I moved my mouth as close to his ear as possible and whispered, "Sorry, big guy, I actually prefer pussy."

"You're lying," he growled and nipped at my earlobe.

"Batta!" someone shouted from down the hall.

Upon hearing his name, he immediately released my wrists and stepped away from me. "Go back to your room," he instructed.

"What's the matter, big guy? Can't handle the heat?" I smirked and licked my lips.

"I'm not the one who'll get burned."

Just as he started to lean closer, someone called his name again. "Fuck!" he bit out and pushed off the wall. Without another word, he turned and disappeared down the hall.

15

BATTA

Searing pain pierced my back. Once. Twice. I couldn't breathe.

"You're disappointing me, Trey." The pain of those words coming from my mother hurt more than the physical pain consuming me. "Why are you acting like this?"

"Their secrets and lies are going to get us killed. Just like Sarah's secrets and lies got you killed."

I felt her hand move from my shoulder to my cheek. I couldn't see her, but I could hear her, and I could feel her. "Oh, my sweet boy, you've got it all wrong."

"How? No one knew about her husband, and he killed you. If we knew, you and Dad would both be here with me."

"We did know. The club tried to help her, but that's ultimately how he found her."

"What?" I asked in disbelief.

"She told me and your father everything. We just didn't tell you. We didn't want you to be worried. I'm so sorry."

"She didn't lie?"

"No, Trey. She didn't. Stop blaming her for something that never happened."

"Is she there? Can you tell her I'm sorry?"

"Not Sarah. Tatum."

I bolted upright, covered in sweat and out of breath. I'd dreamed of Mom many times over the years, but it was usually a memory that played out or some other sequence of events that made no sense. This particular dream felt real, like I was really talking to my mom.

"Batta!" Grant shouted as he pounded on my door. "Church!"

I wiped the sweat from my face and got my ass out of bed. If Copper was calling Church first thing in the morning in the middle of the week, something was up. It'd only been two days since the wreck, so I hoped it was related to that and not something new we needed to deal with.

"The driver of the vehicle was identified as Luther De Santis." Copper held his hand up to keep everyone quiet while he continued. "He's the younger brother of the guy Bronze fought to win the gym, Dez De Santis."

"That can't be a coincidence," I observed.

"It's not. According to the medical examiner, Luther had a recently healed bullet wound to his right shoulder."

Exactly where Tatum shot the man who ran away the night Bronze and I were attacked.

My chest tightened as I waited to hear more.

"So, this is one of the fuckers who tried to kill me and Batta?" Bronze asked.

"Looks like it," Copper said.

"Do we know what their motive was?" I asked.

"I have a pretty good idea," Copper said. "Spazz did a little digging, and it turns out Dez took one too many hits to the head. Apparently, he used to be a legit fighter, but after a particular match ended in a knockout that left him in a coma for three days, no doctor would give him medical clearance to fight again."

"So, he joined the underground circuit," Bronze said knowingly.

"Right. Given his history, it was only a matter of time before he took a devastating blow. Since that happened during his fight with

Bronze, he's the one who got blamed," Copper explained.

"Blamed for what?" I asked.

"Like I said, Dez shouldn't have been fighting in the first place. But, after Bronze knocked him out, he was in such bad shape even the underground fighting ring wouldn't let him fight. Dez supported himself and his younger brother with the money he won from the matches. In other words, his younger brother was pissed because his free ride was suddenly gone."

I sat there in stunned silence for several minutes. And then I exploded. I shoved away from the table and stood so fast my chair landed on the floor with a resounding smack. "You're telling me this little motherfucker tried to kill me and Bronze because his lazy ass didn't want to get a job?" I roared. "How would killing us change that?"

Tiny shrugged, seemingly not bothered by my outburst. "Maybe he was hoping to get three hot meals a day and a place to sleep for free." When we all looked at Tiny like he'd lost his damn mind, he added, "You know, jail."

"Are you fucking serious right now?"

"Sit down!" Copper bellowed. "And shut the

fuck up, Tiny." Copper pinched the bridge of his nose and inhaled deeply, trying to gather some patience. "He's dead, so it doesn't really fucking matter." Then, he swore under his breath and slammed his fist on the table. "I knew getting that gym was too easy."

Bronze reached over and squeezed Copper's shoulder. "Don't do that, brother. What's done is done, and everything's good now."

"Are we sure everything's good now? No disrespect, Prez, but your explanation was what you thought happened, which may or may not be what really happened," I carefully pointed out.

"You're right, and that's why I asked Spazz to look into the other man who entered the ring during the fight. Turns out, that was the man Tatum shot and killed the night you and Bronze were attacked. So, yeah, I feel confident in saying we're in the clear now."

I nodded in agreement. The two men who attempted to kill us were dead, and the likelihood of Dez being able to come after us was minimal at best. And that's when it hit me.

I blamed Tatum and Josie for the attack. I'm pretty sure we all did. And they had absolutely nothing to do with it.

My throat was suddenly dry, and I felt like shit for the way we'd treated them. "Prez," I rasped. "It wasn't their fault."

"Wasn't whose fault?"

"Tatum's and Josie's. They didn't bring trouble to us. We brought it to ourselves."

"And?"

"We need to apologize to them," I blurted.

He grinned. "I already have. Pretty sure you're the only one who's been outwardly hostile to them."

"Shit," I muttered. I had been an asshole to them, but fuck, in my defense, I thought they were the reason I almost lost my life. And even that I could've handled if I'd known why. Not knowing the reason why they were in Devil Springs and what was going on with them was infuriating. Even still, they had secrets, and those secrets could still be a problem for us.

"Now that we know the attack at the gym didn't have anything to do with them, do they still need to stay at the clubhouse?" I asked, trying not to sound hopeful.

"The reason they're here has nothing to do with the attack at the gym. They're here until

Luke has determined whether or not their cover has been blown."

"Wait a minute. If that's the case, then why do they need a babysitter?" I asked. If they were trying to stay hidden, they didn't need someone watching them because they wouldn't try to leave the clubhouse.

"Because you pissed me off by digging into their past and not following orders."

"Understood," I replied and clamped my mouth shut.

"Good. Church dismissed," Copper said and banged his gavel on the table.

I didn't hang around to shoot the shit with the guys like I usually did. Instead, I went straight to the girls' room and knocked on the door.

"Who is it?" Tatum asked in a sing-song voice.

"Batta."

Silence.

I knocked again.

"Who is it?" she sang.

"Batta."

Silence.

Fuck it. I reached for the doorknob, happy to find it unlocked, and pushed the door open.

"What in the hell are you doing?" I blurted.

Josie was on the floor on her back with her legs and arms extended toward the ceiling. Tatum was facing Josie and holding on to her hands while her shoulders rested on the soles of Josie's feet and the rest of her body curved into a backbend suspended in midair.

"AcroYoga. Now, shush it, you're making ripples in my inner peace pond," she snapped. Then, I shit you not, the woman started slowly chanting in a deep tone, "Ohm. Cream of Sum Yum Gai. Ohm." Josie started to giggle. Tatum huffed and, with what appeared to be no effort whatsoever, she pushed off of Josie's feet and gracefully landed in front of me.

"Oh, biker babysitter, did you come to take us to the park? Or maybe the zoo?" she asked excitedly.

Fuck, she wasn't going to make it easy on me, but I had to do it. Clearing my throat, I stood tall and looked her in the eyes, "I came to apologize for the way I've treated the two of you. I learned today that the attempt on my life had nothing to do with you. I blamed you when I should've thanked you for saving my life, as well as my friend's life. I hope you can find it in yourselves to forgive me and maybe we could even be friends."

"Okay, stop right there," Tatum said and pressed her hand to my forehead. Then, she leaned forward and inhaled deeply.

"What in the hell are you doing now?" I asked.

She shrugged. "I figured you were either ill or drunk."

"Tatum," Josie scolded and moved to stand in front of her sister. "Thank you for your kind words," she said and extended her hand to me. "My sister doesn't know how to accept compliments or apologies with any semblance of grace. Thankfully, I do." She smiled and briefly shook my hand. "Now, Tatum, give him a smile and kindly shake his hand."

I chuckled when Tatum petulantly stuck her hand out to shake mine. "You ladies let one of the other brothers know if you need anything. I'm officially off babysitting duty, and I'm going to celebrate." If I hadn't glanced over my shoulder as I was leaving, I would've missed seeing Tatum's face fall, before it morphed into a mask of fury.

16

TATUM

Fuck him and his asshole self. As long as I didn't have to listen to him "celebrating," he could go fuck a hole in the wall or drink himself into a coma for all I cared. His half-assed apology had me fuming.

As soon as he left the room, I grabbed my phone and called Luke. I needed to know what information suddenly had the bikers seeing us in a new light.

"Johnson," he answered.

"Why do you do that when you know it's me calling?"

"Because it's one of the only ways I know how to irritate you," he chirped.

"Whatever. What info did the bikers get today

that would've cleared me and Josie in their eyes?" I asked without preamble.

"They identified the driver who was killed in the car accident in front of the clubhouse the other day. It was the man who ran away from the gym after you shot him," he explained.

"Well, who was it?" I asked impatiently.

"Luther De Santis, twenty-four years old. Single. No children. One older sibling, Dez De Santis," Luke rattled off information I knew he was reading from a computer screen.

"Motive?"

Luke cleared his throat. "Beef with the club."

"Beef? Did you just say beef?" I teased.

He completely ignored me and continued. "I was going to call you later when I was certain, but with this new information, if everything else checks out, you and Josie can return to the safe house tomorrow and resume your regular work routine the day after."

"Really?" I squealed in excitement.

"I'll let you know for sure later tonight or first thing in the morning."

Once I ended the call with Luke, I turned to tell Josie the good news. "There's a possibility we can leave in the morning."

"What?" Josie asked, not sounding happy in the least. "Where would we go?"

"Back to the safe house. We'd continue setting up the bookstore and move forward with our original plan."

"I don't know if that's a good idea," she whispered.

"Why not? Those men weren't after us. They were after the bikers, because of some problem they had with them. There's really no reason for us to be here."

"If Cristofano was able to find me here, anyone else can, too."

"Cristofano didn't find you," I pointed out. "He may have thought he found me, but I've disappeared, and a lovely little cyber trail was planted to lead him away from here."

"I don't know…" she trailed off.

"Think about it and let me know how you feel in the morning. If you're still not okay with the plan, we'll come up with one that you do feel comfortable with," I promised.

"Thank you, Tatum."

"Hey, I learned a long time ago to listen when someone says they have a bad feeling. I'd rather take unnecessary precautions than not take necessary ones. Now, how about we go get something to eat? Audrey's starting to get mouthy again."

After dinner, Josie was still a ball of nerves and in much need of some alcohol. When I went to the bar to get her a drink, the bartender was a girl I hadn't seen before. "Hi, I'm Tatum," I introduced and extended my hand.

"Hello, my name's Heidi," she said and glanced around the empty room. "Uh, are you here with someone?"

I snorted. "My sister and I are being held here against our wills. This is the day they let us out for food, and I saw an opportunity to get some alcohol for us, so I took it."

Heidi gasped in horror. "She's just fucking with you," Batta said from behind me. "She's a guest, so you can serve her and Josie whatever they want."

Heidi laughed nervously. "Oh, okay, well, what can I get you?"

"I'm guessing you don't have a drink menu."

"Give them each a BWOL," Batta said.

"A what?" I asked.

"A BWOL. Stands for Blackwings Old Lady.

It's a drink that Layla concocted. Trust me, it's good."

Heidi returned with two glasses that were either extra-large shot glasses or extra-small drinking glasses. "Um, is a B-WOL a shot or a drink?"

Heidi fidgeted with her hands and Batta shrugged. "We're not sure. I've seen some shoot it and some drink it."

Fuck it. I picked up one of the glasses and tossed it back. "Damn, that's good stuff," I said and immediately downed the other glass. "Two more, please."

When Heidi refilled the glasses, I thanked her and returned to our table. "I don't know what this is, but it's fucking good," I told Josie and placed one of the glasses in front of her.

She picked it up and tentatively took a sip. "Mmm, this is good," she said and followed up with two larger sips. I decided to sip mine as well since I'd already downed two glasses of the liquid goodness.

Once Josie finished hers, I threw back the rest of mine and stood to go back to the bar to get two more before calling it quits for the night. Josie was the very essence of a lightweight, and I didn't like to overdo it with alcohol, especially when I was on an assignment.

I'd taken two steps away from our table when my eyes landed on a woman who looked somewhat familiar to me. I probably could have placed her if she wasn't standing so close to Batta that she was practically raping his bicep with her boobs. Somehow, I managed to maintain a mask of indifference while approaching the bar and asked for not one, not two, but four more drinks—one for Josie and three for me.

"You sure you're okay, Trey? You've seemed off the past few weeks," the arm-raping hussy said while she ran her whore fingers over "Trey's" cheek.

"Here you go," Heidi said, drawing my attention back to her just in the nick of time before I was caught mean-mugging Batta and his guest.

I quickly downed two of the drinks and pushed the glasses back to Heidi. "Thanks, hot stuff," I said with a wink.

On the walk back to our table, I felt the alcohol start to hit me. "Here's your drink," I slurred and slapped my hand over my mouth.

Josie threw her head back and cackled,

drawing the attention of everyone in the room. "Oh, Tatum, you're drunk."

"I am not," I hissed. "Now, shut up and leave your drink so we can finish. Fuck, I mean, finish your drink so we can leave."

"What? Why? I'm having fun," she protested through her laughter.

"Well, I'm not," I grumbled and took another sip.

Josie glanced back at the bar. "Oh, I see," she said.

"Not another word."

"Okay, I won't say another word. Let's take these drinks back to our room so you can sit in there and imagine what's going on out here. Better yet, maybe we can get that tech guy to put the camera feed on our TV so you can livestream the canoodling."

Finishing the rest of my drink, I slammed the glass down on the table and stormed out of the common room. What in the hell was wrong with me? I had no claim on Batta, aka the man who lets the sluts call him Trey. He could do whatever or whomever he wanted. I didn't want him, and I was most definitely not one of those women who wanted a man to want me, even though I didn't want him.

I pushed through the back door and deeply inhaled the crisp night air. Then, I started to pace.

I was not jealous.

I was not jealous.

I was so fucking jealous I could taste it.

And it was pissing me off. Royally. I wanted to hit something, but there was nothing in my vicinity that I could punch without seriously messing up my hand. That man was under my skin, and I needed to get him out before I landed my ass in hot water.

I opened my mouth to scream in frustration but froze when I heard the back door open. I knew who it was without even turning around to look. "What?" I asked harshly.

"Come 'ere," he rumbled.

"No."

"Tatum, turn the fuck around, and come here," he demanded.

When I turned around, he was standing there with his muscular arms crossed over his chest waiting for me to come to him. I kept my eyes locked on his as I slowly shook my head. He smirked and took one step toward me. Shrugging,

I took one step in his direction. We matched each other's steps until I was within his reach. Then, his arm shot out and wrapped around my neck. With one firm yank, our bodies slammed together while his lips crashed into mine and I saw stars. His hand tangled in my hair while he devoured my mouth in a ferocious kiss.

"I want you so fucking bad," he mumbled against my skin.

"Then have me."

"Oh, I fucking will," he vowed. "As soon as you're sober."

I broke the kiss and reached for the door, pulling him along behind me. "What're you doing?"

"Going to eat some damn bread or something so I can ride you like I stole you without you feeling guilty."

He laughed and pulled me back against his chest. His hands came around and cupped my full breasts. "I can't wait to play with these. I'm going to suck on your nipples until they're nice and red, then I'm going to watch them bounce to the beat of my cock pounding into you." With a final squeeze, he said, "Go wait in my room while I get you something to eat."

I entered his room and had no idea what to do with myself. Should I sit in the chair? Stand by the door? Display myself in a sexy pose across the bed? And then I got a little pissed at myself. I was not a woman who struggled with confidence. I was who I was, and you either liked me or you didn't; either way, it didn't much matter to me.

With that decided, I kicked my boots off, climbed onto his bed, and propped myself up against the headboard with a few pillows. He entered the room a few minutes later with a plate full of sandwiches in one hand and two bottles of water in the other.

"Were you planning on inviting guests to join us?" I asked and nodded to the plate of food.

He shrugged. "I'm hungry, and it takes more than one little sandwich to fuel this body. Based on your physique, I would say the same is true for you."

"Yeah," I said and grabbed a sandwich. "I have to stay in shape for my—." Fuck! I shoved half the sandwich into my mouth to stop myself from telling him things he didn't need to know. After swallowing, I added, "Sorry. I have to stay in shape for my low insurance rate."

"Really? That's the best you could come up with."

"Apparently," I muttered.

"I don't like secrets," he mumbled.

"And I don't particularly like keeping them," I retorted.

He seemed surprised by my response. "Then, why do you do it?"

"It's part of my job," I answered simply.

He sighed. "I don't know what you do exactly, but I know you have some kind of working relationship with Luke Johnson. I won't try to figure it out on my own, but you can tell me."

"That's just it. I can't tell you any more than you already know. Not right now," I confessed.

"You're undercover," he mused.

I arched an eyebrow. "Didn't I just say I couldn't tell you anything?"

"Did that sound like a question?"

I smiled and shook my head. "Smart-ass."

"Hello, Pot. I'm Kettle," he joked and took a bite of his sandwich. "Tell me something about you."

I arched an eyebrow. "Thought you already knew everything about me."

"You're not going to make this easy on me, are you?" he chuckled.

Grinning, I shook my head. "It's not in my nature."

"I can see that. Okay, fine, where are you from?"

I swallowed the bite of food in my mouth and answered honestly. "I grew up in Virginia Beach. Technically, I still live there, but I travel a lot for work. What about you? Are you from Devil Springs?"

"Born and raised here and I have no plans of leaving."

"Do you have family here?" I asked. I already knew the answer, but I wanted to see what he would say.

"The club is my family," he said sharply. After a brief pause, he added, "My mother died when I was sixteen. My dad's in prison, but you already knew that."

"I'm sorry," I apologized. "I shouldn't have asked."

"It's fine. I'm not ashamed of it. It sucks that he's not here with me, and I think he got a shit deal, but I understand why he did what he did," he explained.

I glanced down at the sandwich in my hands. "Yeah, I wish my parents were still here, too. I assume you know what happened to them."

"You want to talk about it?" he asked carefully.

"There's not much to tell. A little over five years ago, they went on a trip for their thirtieth wedding anniversary, and their cabin caught on fire. They weren't able to make it out."

"Well, that was a complete buzz kill," Batta said and sat up.

"Wasn't that the point?" I joked.

He snorted. "No, the point was to sober you up."

I shrugged. "Potato. Potahto."

He grinned. "Tomato. Tomahto."

I started laughing, and before I knew it, I was on my side, clutching my stomach in a fit of giggles that would not relent. It wasn't anything exceptionally funny, but I couldn't get myself under control.

Batta's hand landed on my jaw and startled me out of my laughter. "You're a beautiful woman, but damn, you light up the whole fucking room when you laugh," he said softly.

"I'm a little ray of sunshine," I blurted, using sarcasm because I was unsure of what to say.

"You're something," he murmured right before his lips were on mine, gentle at first, but quickly becoming more intense.

A moment of clarity broke through my lust-induced haze and I broke the kiss while pushing against his chest. "Before this goes any further, I need to know a few things."

"I don't fuck without a condom," he said instantly.

"Neither do I, but that's not what I meant," I said and swallowed thickly. I didn't want to be that woman, but I also didn't want to be the other woman. "The woman, at the bar. Is she—"

"She's a good friend. We dated for a while, but we had a platonic relationship for most of it. I haven't slept with her or anyone in over six months. She feels bad because we broke up a few hours before I got shot."

She didn't look like she was just a friend with the way she was rubbing her tits all over his arm, but I wasn't going to point that out. Batta laughed and traced a circle around my lips with his finger. "This little grimace you've got going on is pretty cute. I rather like this softer side of you."

I reached down and grabbed a handful of his crotch, and what a handful it was, but I didn't let that distract me. "Did you just call me soft?"

"Hell, no," he said vehemently. "I said softer. Your softer side is still harder than most men's." He leaned forward and trailed kisses up my neck to the shell of my ear. "Do you want to know the real reason Kennedy and I are just friends?"

Something about the way he asked made me unsure of my answer. "Do I?"

He moved his big body over mine, all the while I still had his balls and part of his dick in my grasp. One hand slid up my torso and wrapped around my neck firmly. "I don't make love, sugar tits. I fuck. And I fuck hard. She couldn't handle me."

I grinned. "I can assure you, big guy, that won't be a problem for me."

"Let go of my balls and put your hands above your head," he commanded. Commanded. No one had ever spoken to me like that in bed, and I kind of liked it, but there was no way I was going to do what he said.

Grinning mischievously, I pushed against his chest. "Hold that thought, big guy." When he moved back, I sat up and removed the gun from the small of my back as well as the one strapped to my ankle. Then, I pulled one from the pocket of my tactical pants. Once all were placed on the nightstand, I returned to my previous position and let him think I was complacent by placing my hands above my head.

With a sly smile, he straddled my waist and reached for my belt. "Call me Trey."

"I thought your name was Jace Ryder Wild."

"It is. Jace Ryder Wild III. Trey's a nickname for a third-generation son. Everyone else calls me Batta. You can call me Trey."

While he explained and focused on getting into my pants, I planted my feet on the bed and bucked my hips upward. At the same time the palm of my hand forcefully met the underside of his chin, effectively tossing him off of me. "Sorry, Trey, I don't take orders from anyone."

With a feral growl, he reached up and tore my tank top from my body with his bare hands. "You want to play, baby girl? Let's play." Reversing our positions, he gathered my wrists in one hand and divested me of my pants with the other. I twisted my body and struggled against him, but I was trapped between his massive thighs.

The distinct snick of a blade locking into

place sounded in the room before I caught sight of the glint from the metal. My eyes narrowed, and I renewed my efforts to get out of his grasp. I didn't sign up to become minced meat at the hands of a rabid biker. "If you cu—"

My words died on my lips when he slid the blade underneath the center of my bra. With a swift jerk of his wrist, the material separated and fell uselessly to the side. He didn't stop to look at what he uncovered before he tossed the knife aside and ripped my thong from my body. The flimsy strings easily gave way to his strength.

With my wrists still secured in his unforgiving grip, he placed his knees between my legs and pushed my thighs as wide as they could go, making it extremely difficult for me to find any kind of footing.

He ran his finger over my bare mound and along the inside of my thighs. Every part of me ached for more and, despite my efforts to hide my desire, he knew. "Look at that pretty, wet pussy just begging to be filled." He ran one finger through my slit and held his glistening finger up for me to see. Then, he unceremoniously shoved two, maybe three, fingers inside of me and started pumping them so vigorously it felt like they were vibrating.

"Trey," I gasped. I'd never felt anything like what he was doing to my body. And I decidedly did not want him to stop. Ever. "Oh, shit, I'm going to come."

"No the fuck you're not," he informed me and promptly removed his fingers.

I groaned at the loss but refused to give him any more than that, even though my body was aching with need.

He scowled down at me before he flipped me onto my stomach and raised my arms over my head. Using the remnants of my bra, he started to tie my hands together. "Wait! Hold up."

He relaxed his hold on my wrists but didn't fully release them. "You scared, Queen Badass?"

I snorted. "Not at all. But I'm on an assignment. I need your word that you'll let me go if duty calls."

"If I say yes, will you behave?"

"Likely not, but I really don't like breaking necks with my ankles, so can we come to some kind of agreement here?"

His eyes glazed over with desire. "You've done that?"

"Focus, Batman."

"If something happens, I'll cut you loose," he promised.

"Okie dokie. Carry on."

With that, he secured my wrists to the headboard before he flipped me back over and hovered over me with a devious grin on his face. Without uttering a word, he studied my eyes for a few moments before he moved off the bed and got something from his dresser.

Instead of climbing between my legs, he walked to the side of the bed and grabbed my ankle. When he slipped a loop of rope over my foot, I opened my mouth to protest. Clearly anticipating my response, he picked up my shredded panties and shoved them into my mouth to silence me.

I was still trying to figure out what in the hell he was doing to me when he finished securing my ankles to the headboard, leaving me folded in half and completely exposed for whatever he wanted to do to me. I'd be lying if I said I wasn't a little wary on some level, but the thrill of it all far outweighed any minuscule amount of fear I felt.

"Look at you," he mused. "All helpless and spread out for me with your cunt dripping all over my sheets. I can't decide if I want to fuck it with my fingers, my tongue, or my cock."

I moaned as my core clenched at nothing but air. At that point, I didn't care which one he picked, as long as he picked one and did it quickly.

He flashed me a wicked grin. "Or maybe I'll let your naughty pussy suffer and fuck those tits of yours. I'd love to come all over your smart-ass fucking mouth."

Reaching behind his head, he grasped the collar of his shirt and pulled it off in one fluid movement. Damn, the man was nothing but a solid block of ripped muscle. He watched me watch him as he undid his jeans and let them drop to the floor, followed by his boxer briefs, leaving him standing completely naked with the large weapon he was packing proudly on display. I briefly wondered if that was how he got his road name.

My mouth watered as he ran his hand over his hardened length and climbed onto the bed between my widely splayed legs. Never taking his eyes off of mine, he leaned forward and captured my left nipple in his mouth, sucking so hard my back bowed off the bed. He continued to torture my left nipple with his mouth while his fingers pinched and rolled the right one. I moaned and tried to wiggle my hips while my pussy clenched with need. He chuckled against my skin and moved his mouth to my other breast to give it the same torturous attention.

I wanted his mouth on mine. I wanted him to fuck me. I wanted him to fill me with his fingers again. I wanted him to make me come. And I was ever so grateful for the makeshift gag in my mouth. It was preventing me from begging him to fulfill any or all of my wishes, and from begging him to let me run my hands over his chiseled chest, to let me kiss every square inch of his body, to take his huge cock in my mouth and suck until he came down my throat.

As if reading my thoughts, he released my breast with a pop and pulled my panties from my mouth. Heaving and panting, I felt like I was going to explode from the desire building within me.

Grinning at me, he sat back on his heels and held a foil packet up for me to see. Ripping it open with his teeth, he tossed the wrapper aside and made quick work of rolling the condom down his shaft.

He moved closer, his nose mere millimeters away from mine, the warm puffs of his breath gently caressing my lips. All I had to do was slightly lift my head and I could have his lips, but I refused to give in more than I already had.

When his big hand landed on my pussy in a stinging slap, my head shot forward as my body tried to curl upward, and my lips crashed into his in what immediately turned into an all-consuming, frenzied kiss. Our tongues battled for dominance as we tried to devour each other. I strained against the ropes holding me in place as I tried to get closer to him.

He landed another hard slap between my legs before he thrust his condom-covered cock inside of me. I sucked in a sharp breath at the delicious burn as my body stretched to accommodate him.

He didn't wait for me to adjust. He wrapped his hands around my thighs and immediately began thrusting into me like a rabid beast. My mouth opened in a silent scream as I came so hard I swear my heart stopped for several beats.

I finally gasped in a breath when he landed a stinging swat to my thigh. "Holy." Gasp. "Shit." Gasp.

Before I could get my bearings, he sliced

through the ropes securing my ankles to the headboard and flipped me onto my stomach. With my arms still bound above me, there was little I could do to adjust my position, which clearly wasn't a concern for Trey as he didn't pause before grabbing my hips and lifting me to my knees. With my ass hoisted in the air, he slammed back inside of me.

He fucked like a machine. He was thrusting into me with such force that uncontrollable grunts escaped me each time his hips came forward and pressed my torso down into the mattress.

With a handful of my hair, he yanked my head back with just enough force to make my scalp tingle with the barest hint of pain. "I want to hear you scream my name when you come."

Just when I thought he was giving me all he had, he proved me wrong. He let go of my hair and grabbed my hips, using them to pull me back as he slammed forward. Our bodies were coming together with such force that I knew I'd feel bruised for days afterward with every move I made. And that thought was what sent me spiraling into another epic climax.

"Say it," he demanded with a slap to my ass.

"Trey!" I screamed. "Oh, fuck, fuck, fuck. Trey! Don't stop. Please don't stop."

And he didn't stop until several minutes, maybe hours, later when he finally reached his own climax.

When his sweat-soaked body dropped to the bed, he reached over and placed his big hand on my cheek. I waited patiently for a few minutes, but when he didn't show any indication of moving, I asked, "Can you untie my wrists?"

He sat up and let his eyes roam over my body before he got to his feet. "No, but I'll let you have some water before I eat your pussy and fuck another part of you."

17

BATTA

I startled awake from a deep sleep, unsure of what had woken me. When I sat up, my eyes landed on Tatum as she pulled her pants up over her firm, bare ass. "Get the fuck up!" she whisper-shouted and started pulling open the drawers of my dresser. "Shirts! Where the fuck are your shirts?"

"Third one down," I told her and reached for my own jeans. "What's going on?"

"Shhh!" she hissed and pulled one of my black T-shirts over her head. Pointing toward the common room, she informed me, "Something's going on out there. I've got to get to Josie." With that, she shoved one of her guns in the back of her pants, picked up the other two, and made sure the coast was clear before she darted across the hall.

With my door left partially open, I could hear disgruntled male voices coming from the common room. Grabbing my bat, I stomped down the hall ready to bust the bones of whoever caused my woman to cover her luscious naked body and leave my bed. My woman? I nodded to myself in affirmation because that's exactly what she was. From the moment our lips touched for the first time, I knew she was and always would be mine.

"What in the actual mother fuck is going on out here?" I roared when I saw Grant and Coal using their bodies to physically block the front door. Heidi was cowering behind the bar, quietly crying. I briefly thought about sending her to Tatum's room. I knew she would protect her if she didn't shoot her first, which she probably would. "Go lock yourself in my room, sweetheart. Don't open the door for anyone other than a brother."

She nodded and mouthed, "Thank you," before she ran down the hall.

"I know she's in there!" a man shouted. "Let

me in! You can't keep her from me!" He sounded desperate, borderline manic, and that translated to dangerous for anyone in his path.

I continued moving toward Grant and Coal and made my presence known with each step I took. "Who in the hell do you think you are coming to our clubhouse in the middle of the damn night demanding to see any-fucking-body?"

"You! You motherfucker! I know you're hiding her! She's mine!" he furiously shouted as he broke through Grant and Coal with a sudden burst of anger and barreled right for me.

Before my mind even registered what was happening, I raised my bat and swung it at the man's head, making contact with a resounding crack. No one was coming into my home and hurting my family on my watch. He dropped to the ground like a sack of bricks just as a horrified scream filled the air.

"Noooo! Cristofano!" Josie shrieked and ran for the unconscious man.

Tatum caught up with her before she made it even a third of the way across the room and tackled her to the ground. She pulled Josie's arms behind her back and held them with one hand while she covered her mouth with the other. Readjusting her grip, she hoisted Josie from the floor and physically removed her from the room while Josie sobbed hysterically, never taking her eyes off Cristofano.

Bronze materialized from the hallway, took one look at the scene, and let out a stream of expletives before he started barking orders. "You two, restrain him and take him out back. Batta, make sure the gates are locked and do a quick perimeter check," he said and put his phone to his ear.

"Need you here, now, brother. Trouble just forced its way through our front door," I heard him say as I was heading out the front door.

The car I assumed to be Cristofano's was haphazardly parked in the forecourt and luckily empty. However, there was no way for me to lock the gate because, presumably, Cristofano had seen the gate as optional and drove right through it.

I stepped beyond the broken gate and looked for any cars parked on the side of the road. Thankfully, it appeared that Cristofano had made the trip on his own. I turned to go back inside just as a minivan sped through the gate and hit the road in a spray of dust and gravel.

"Fucking fuck!" I yelled into the night and swung my bat at the mangled gate. I started to run for my bike, but I knew there was no way I would be able to catch up with them since I had no idea where they would go.

"Batta!" Bronze called as he stepped outside. When he saw me, he held his hand up and tossed a set of keys to me. "Move his car around back."

Without a word, I slid into Cristofano's fancy-ass car and swore when I banged my knees on the dash and the damn steering wheel. When I moved the seat back, the edge of a manila envelope appeared from beneath the seat. I pulled it from its hiding place and quickly moved the car behind one of the sheds on the backside of the clubhouse.

Since Cristofano came onto our property uninvited and made a great show of disrespect, I treated him just like I would any other threat. I thoroughly searched through his belongings, including ripping open the envelope and upending its contents in the passenger seat.

Nothing, absolutely nothing, would have prepared me for the papers that fell onto the smooth leather. Pictures. Dozens of pictures. Of

Josie. Of Josie and Cristofano. Together. And they looked like a couple. A happy couple.

"What the fuck?" I breathed and continued to flip through photo after photo. I knew she was fucking lying when Copper asked her if she knew Luca. There was no way Tatum didn't know who the Peccatis were if her own fucking sister was in a relationship with Luca's second-in-command.

When I shoved the photos back into the envelope, I noticed a few pieces of paper were still inside. Hastily, I yanked them out and scanned over the handwritten words but none of it made any sense to me. It appeared to be mostly dates and times with a few cities listed at the bottom.

I didn't have time to try to figure out the connection, so I folded the envelope, shoved it into my pocket, and exited the car. But, before I went back inside, I swung my bat at each door, the trunk, and the hood. Satisfied with my work, I propped my bat on my shoulder and walked through the back door, whistling a jaunty tune as I went.

"I was about to come look for you. Thought you might've been taken out by a speeding minivan," Bronze joked, though I could hear the hint of worry in his voice.

"Found something in Cristofano's car," I spat and tossed the envelope onto the table.

Bronze's brow furrowed. "You okay?"

I nodded my head to the envelope. "Open it."

His reaction didn't disappoint. "What in the fresh hell is this? That's Josie! And what is this shit?"

"What is what shit?" Copper asked as he stormed into the room.

Bronze tossed the pictures to him. "See for yourself, brother."

Copper swiped them from the table and dropped into his chair. "You have got to be fucking kidding me! Where did these come from?"

"I found them under the front seat of Cristofano's car."

"What the fuck is this?" Copper asked, holding up the handwritten list of dates and times. "Was he tracking her?"

Judge walked in looking like a pissed off bear. Tiny and Spazz entered right behind him with equal looks of irritation on their faces. Copper didn't waste any time and quickly filled them in on the night's events.

Judge leaned back and crossed his arms over

his chest. "Are you saying Cristofano is who Tatum and Josie are running from?"

"It can't be him," Spazz interjected. "Josie was married to Sheldon Morgan. They were married for three years before he died a few months ago."

"So what? She could've been having an affair with Cristofano," Judge countered.

"Josie and Sheldon lived in Virginia Beach. Cristofano lives in Cedar Valley. It doesn't make sense for her to 'run' to a place that's closer to the person she's trying to get away from."

Judge shrugged. "Maybe. Or it could've been a strategic move. Because, like you said, it wouldn't make sense."

"Only a handful of people know the truth, and none of them are in this room. So, let's stop wasting time speculating and figure out the best way to handle the shitstorm that just blew our way," Copper stated.

"Unless we kill him and hide the body, we're going to have to speak with his boss. Assuming you don't want to kill Cristofano, would you rather talk to Luca now or in the morning?" Bronze asked.

Copper opened his mouth to speak but was

interrupted by his phone buzzing. He glanced at the screen and grinned. "He's awake. Let's go have a chat, boys."

We entered the shed to find Cristofano fighting with everything he had to get out of his restraints. "Let me go, you motherfuckers!" he snarled.

"Tell me something," Copper started. "What in the hell made you think you could come here and start giving orders? This is my clubhouse, and these are my men. You don't mean anything to any of us here," Copper said vehemently.

Cristofano's head shot up and his eyes widened when they landed on Copper. Surprisingly, his lips instantly clamped shut.

"Oh, now you have nothing to say?"

"Where is she?" he gritted out.

"Where is who?" Copper taunted.

"Adrianna. Where is she? What did you do with her?" he asked, almost frantically.

Copper pulled a picture from the pocket of his cut and held it up for Cristofano to see. "Who is this woman?"

"Why are you doing this? For money? I have plenty of it. Just give her back to me." The sheer desperation in his voice almost had me feeling sorry for him.

"Answer my question," Copper demanded.

"Adrianna!" he screamed. "That's my Adrianna! So help me, if you don't give her back to me, I will slice the throat of every man in your club and dance as your blood rains down on me."

Copper glanced at me over his shoulder. "How hard did you hit him?"

I shrugged. "Same as I always do."

Copper turned his attention to Grant and Coal. "Either one of you get his cell phone?"

Coal produced it from his pocket and handed it over to Copper. "Thanks, man. I want both of you on guard duty until I say otherwise." With that, we followed him back into the clubhouse, where he stopped by the bar and grabbed a bottle of whiskey on his way to Church.

"Spazz, see what you can find on an Adrianna tied to the Peccatis."

"Already on it, Prez," Spazz replied while his fingers rapidly clicked keys on his laptop.

Copper took a swig of whiskey straight from the bottle and passed it to Bronze, who took a drink and passed it on to the next brother. "I knew they were running from something," Copper started. "Luke straight-up told me he couldn't give me any details on their situation when he asked for our help, which I understood and agreed to. But a potential war with the Peccatis changes things."

"Agreed. How do you want to handle this?" Bronze asked.

"We're going to wait," he said and took another pull from the bottle.

"Wait? For what?" I asked.

"For the phone to ring. You know good and well Tatum called Luke the second they hit the road, so he'll be calling any minute now. And at some point, Luca will realize Cristofano is missing and start looking for him."

"You don't think we should call Luca and tell him to come get his man?" Judge asked.

"No, I don't. They need to know we won't tolerate this kind of bullshit from anyone, no matter what kind of connections they have," Copper said vehemently.

Judge pushed back from the table. "I'm going to call River and let her know I won't be home tonight."

"Might be a good idea to have all the girls

spend the day at your mom's house," Copper suggested.

"You think that's necessary?" Judge asked, his face full of concern.

"We don't know what we're dealing with. I'd rather know for sure they were safe instead of risking it." Copper redirected his attention to Spazz. "You got anything?"

"Maybe," he mumbled. "Sheldon Morgan was supposedly shot and killed in his basement during a home invasion. But, I can't find a death certificate for him. Also, I found one article that had a link to the original story before it was updated. The original story says two people in the home were shot during a domestic dispute, and two bodies covered with sheets were removed from the house."

I shook my head and looked down at the table. "None of this makes any fucking sense."

The sound of Copper's phone ringing caused the room to fall silent. Copper put it on speaker and placed it on the table in front of him. "Luke, what a surprise."

"I highly doubt that. Have you contacted Luca yet?" Luke asked in a tone I hadn't heard from him before.

"We haven't contacted anyone at this point."

"Good," he said and exhaled slowly. "I know you want answers, but I can't give you any. But I do still need your help."

"You serious right now? I've got an angry Italian tied up in my shed threatening to kill my entire club if I don't hand over the woman we know as Josie but he seems to think is Adrianna. And you wanna tell me why Cristofano has pictures of him and Josie? Pictures that indicate they clearly know each other and were likely in a relationship together."

"Fuck!" Luke swore. "Where are those pictures now?"

"On the table in front of me," Copper answered.

"Destroy them."

"Excuse me?"

"Destroy them. Burn them. Flush them. I don't give a shit, just get rid of them!" Luke shouted. "Fucking hell. Did he actually see her?"

"Who?"

"Cristofano. Did he see Josie?"

Copper raised his eyes to me. "I don't think so. He was trying to get in the front door, and when he finally broke through, I knocked him out. Josie did see him, though," I explained.

Luke sighed. "Yeah, I know she did. Like I said, I can't give you any solid answers; but I can assure you, Luca and Cristofano are not a threat to your club."

"Again, the angry Italian says otherwise," Copper retorted.

"The angry Italian won't be a problem as soon as his boss has a word with him."

Copper sighed. "What kind of help do you need from us?"

"I need to send Tatum back to the clubhouse. Alone. Have her pretend to be seeing one of the brothers. When Luca comes to get Cristofano, let him see Tatum there with someone. If he asks, and he probably will, tell him she's been in town for a few weeks to spend some time with her boyfriend. Make no mention of Josie."

"Give me a minute," Copper said and put the phone on mute. "Let's put it to a vote."

I didn't give a shit how it made me look. I was the first one to vote in favor of having Tatum return to the clubhouse. My eagerness did not go unnoticed as each of my brothers voted the same as me.

After unmuting the phone, Copper asked, "When should we expect Tatum to arrive?"

"Thank you. Your help and cooperation are greatly appreciated and will not be forgotten. Tatum should be back by six o'clock or so."

"What?" I blurted. "Where the fuck did she go?"

"I'm sorry, I'm not at liberty to say," Luke answered automatically.

18

TATUM

"Please don't leave me," Josie begged through her tears.

"You know I don't want to, but I agree with Luke that this is the best way to keep you safe," I reassured her. I had no idea how Cristofano had found us, but he had, and it was by sheer luck that he hadn't seen her. I pulled her in for a hug and whispered, "You know I wouldn't leave you if I didn't think you'd be safe."

She nodded against my shoulder. "I know," she sniffled. "But I don't know these people."

"You can trust them, Josie," I told her and hoped I wasn't lying. Luke vouched for them, and I was in a position where I had to take his word.

"I need to get back or this will all be for naught. So, go inside, and I'll call when I can."

Josie's frail arms tightened around me for a long moment before she released me and stepped back. "Please be careful, Tatum," she whispered.

"I will," I vowed and directed my attention to the two beautiful, blonde women huddled around Josie and the two protective men standing behind them. They looked familiar, really familiar, but I couldn't place them. "Take care of her."

"Nothing will happen to her while she's in our care," the older of the two men promised and, for whatever reason, I believed him.

"Thank you," I said sincerely and slid into the driver's seat without looking back. I wanted to, but I couldn't. Because if I did, I would have shoved Josie into the van and kept on driving, even though I knew she was in the best place she could be.

The drive back to the clubhouse was awful. When I wasn't using every ounce of energy to stay awake, my mind was running wide-open trying to figure out how Cristofano tracked us down. Because if he was able to find us, that meant anyone else could, too. I was desperate to know what he knew, or what he thought he knew.

And I was curious to know how much the bikers had figured out since we'd been gone.

I pulled into the clubhouse and parked the minivan in the exact same place it'd been before I left. Assuming they were expecting me, I didn't bother with knocking and let myself in the front door. Batta was kicked back on one of the sofas with his arms crossed over his broad chest, and he was fast asleep.

I walked over to him and placed my hand on his cheek. "Batta," I said softly.

His beautiful blue eyes fluttered open and promptly narrowed. "I told you to call me Trey."

"Trey," I repeated.

Not one ounce of tension left his face upon my use of his given name. Instead, his glare intensified. "We need to talk."

"I know," I sighed. "But can we do it after I get a few hours of sleep? I'm exhausted and kind of bitchy."

He got to his feet and stood toe-to-toe with me. "I don't like liars."

I dropped my head and stared at my boots. "I don't like lying," I confessed. "I only do it when I have to for my job." I wasn't going to apologize to him because I wasn't sorry. I didn't like lying to him and his friends, but I wasn't sorry for doing it.

"So you do know Luca Peccati?"

I was exhausted and didn't have the energy to argue with him, especially when he already knew some of the truth. "Of course I do. How could I not?"

"Because of who Luca is? Or because your sister was dating Cristofano?"

"What?" I gasped. What did he know?

He held up a picture of Josie and Cristofano. "We were supposed to destroy these, but I kept one because I wanted to see the look on your face when you saw it."

I held his gaze. "Well, you've seen my reaction."

He shook his head and pulled a lighter from his pocket. Seconds later, the photo went up in a flame and he dropped it to the floor, putting it out with his boot.

I waited for more but nothing came. Continuing to avoid his angry eyes, I turned and started down the hall toward the room Josie and I had shared.

"Where in the hell do you think you're going?" he barked.

"I'm going to go lay down and get a few hours of sleep. Like I said, I'm exhausted and kind of bitchy. It's only going to get worse."

When I reached the room we'd been staying in, a large arm slid around my waist and turned me in the opposite direction. "You'll sleep with me," he stated.

With me still in front of him, he turned the knob and pushed his bedroom door open. I was ready to fall face-down into the bed until I saw a woman curled up in his sheets.

"Oh, I don't fucking think so," I snarled as his arms tightened around me.

"Don't start. I sent Heidi in here when everything was happening. I told her not to leave until someone came for her, and I forgot to send someone to get her," he explained.

"Whatever," I snapped. "I'm pissed. You're pissed. Can I just go to the other room and sleep?" I wasn't sure I believed his story about the girl, but I was too tired to push for answers.

Of course, the girl chose that moment to shoot straight up in the bed and look around with fear-filled eyes. "Batta?" she gasped. "Is everything okay?"

"Yeah, Heidi, it's fine now. You can go crash

in the room across the hall if you want," he offered.

"Oh, okay, um, thanks," she stammered. I won't deny being pleased to see that she was fully dressed when she tossed his sheets off and climbed out of the bed. "You're sure it's okay?"

"Yeah, sweetheart," he said and opened the door for her.

"Heidi, what're you still doing here?" Bronze asked, appearing out of nowhere.

"I sent her to my room when the trouble started, and she fell asleep," Batta explained.

"Well, come on, darlin'. You can finish napping in my room," Bronze offered and grabbed her hand. Heidi's cheeks flushed, but she followed him to his room without another word.

Trey turned back to me. "I'm pissed, and I have a lot of questions. I want to fucking believe you, but then more shit happens and all you can say is you can't tell me. So, get your ass in the bed before I spank it."

"I hate to break it to you, Batman, but that threat's not going to work. I like spankings," I said with a sly smile.

"Tatum," he growled.

And I just couldn't. I was tired, upset, and

beyond stressed. "Can I have a hug?" I asked.

"What?"

"A hug. Can I have one?" I asked again, my voice catching in my throat, and I didn't even try to hide it.

"Are you fucking with me right now?"

I looked up and met his sparkling blue eyes as one tear slid down my cheek. "No."

"Yeah, baby," he said softly as realization dawned. "Come 'ere." I snorted when he didn't give me a chance to actually come to him. Instead, he fisted my shirt and pulled me against his chest while his arms surrounded me with the comfort I so desperately needed. "You okay?"

I nodded against his chest even though I wasn't sure that I was. "I'm just worried," I confessed.

"Not much I can say to make you feel better," he said, and I clearly heard what he didn't say—*because I don't know what in the hell is going on.*

He released me after a few moments of blissful silence. I promptly kicked off my boots and stripped out of my pants before climbing into his bed. He stripped down to his boxer briefs and slid into the bed right behind me. "What happened with Cristofano?" I asked.

I felt him shrug. "Nothing yet."

"Yet?"

"Luca hasn't called or come to get him yet."

"He's still here?" I almost shouted.

"I thought you wanted to sleep."

"I do. I just…I didn't think he would still be here. Has he said anything?" I asked. Cristofano could potentially ruin everything with a few choice words.

"He threatened to kill everyone in our club if we didn't hand over Adrianna."

It took everything I had to keep myself from reacting. Forcing myself to remain calm and relaxed, I asked, "Who?"

"Some girl named Adrianna. He seems to think we have her here."

My heart started pounding in my chest, but I was completely unfazed on the outside, or so I hoped. I chuckled. "Why would he think that? Do you guys routinely keep women at your clubhouse?"

"Just you and Josie," he deadpanned.

I didn't know what to say to that, so I chose to say nothing at all and pretended to be asleep. I didn't have to pretend for long.

19

BATTA

It took longer than I expected for Luca Peccati to start looking for his missing man. It was almost noon when Cristofano's cell phone finally rang. Since we were all hanging around the clubhouse waiting for the show to begin, we followed Copper into Church as he answered the phone.

"Thank you for calling the Blackwings Crisis Line. If an associate of yours has gone missing, please press one," Copper said jovially.

"Fuck," Luca cursed. "What did he do?"

"I have to say, Luca, that was not the reaction I was expecting from you."

Luca cleared his throat. "I am aware of his

current problems. What I am not aware of is what kind of trouble he may have caused for you."

"I think it would be best if we discussed this in person."

"Yes, well, that may be in your best interest, but I'm not sure it is in mine," Luca replied.

Copper sighed. "Enough with the formalities, Luca. We just want you to come get your man and have a chat. No trouble."

"Very well. Piero will be accompanying me. We will be leaving within the hour," Luca said and disconnected the call.

Copper picked up his phone, dialed another number, and placed his phone on speaker. "Luke Johnson."

"Copper Black. I just spoke with Luca. He'll be here to get Cristofano in a few hours."

"Good. No matter what either of them say, do not give them any indication anyone other than Tatum has been at the clubhouse, or in Devil Springs for that matter. And, make sure one or both of them see her," Luke instructed.

"You're asking a lot, especially when we don't know what the fuck we're keeping from them," Copper countered.

Luke sighed. "You'll be helping us save countless lives all over the world. Innocent lives."

"Well, I suppose I can't argue with that," Copper muttered.

"Thanks, man. I'll owe you a marker for this," Luke said causing Copper's eyebrows to raise.

"Appreciate it. I'll be in touch if things don't go according to plan." With that, the call ended, and Copper addressed the room. "You all heard that for yourselves. You're free to do what you want for the next two hours, but I want each and every one of you in this clubhouse when Luca arrives."

Sounds of affirmation sounded around the room. As soon as Copper banged his gavel, I got to my feet and headed back to my room to check on Tatum.

Opening the door to my room, I expected her to still be asleep, but my bed was empty. My heart seized in my chest for a brief second before I heard the shower running. Shaking my head to myself for jumping to conclusions, I shamelessly pushed the door open and walked inside the bathroom.

My dick was already half-hard when I stepped inside and pulled my shirt over my head. And it promptly deflated when I heard her sniffle. No longer trying to be covert, I yanked the curtain back and found Tatum slumped against the shower wall with her hands covering her face as she tried to stifle her cries.

Seeing a woman as strong as Tatum breakdown sent my protective instincts into overdrive. "Aw, shit, baby," I rasped and pulled her soaking wet body into my arms. And that's when she did break. The sobs she had been trying to contain broke free and filled the silence surrounding us.

I snagged a towel from the rack and wrapped it around her, hoping it would provide a little warmth. Lightly rubbing her back, I asked, "Is this about Josie?" I felt her nod against my chest as she choked on a sob.

"Talk to me."

"I fucking can't!" she screamed and started to beat her fists against my upper chest. "And I want to talk about it! I need to!"

It wasn't easy for a man like me to remain calm while a woman like her used me as a punching bag. When I'd had enough, I grabbed her wrists and halted her assault. "Tell me what you can."

She shook her head and tried to fight back the tears. "I had to leave her with someone else—someone I don't know! I always have to leave her!"

I pulled her close, kissed the top of her head, and let her cry, or scream, against my chest. There was nothing I could say or do to make the situation better for her. And while it pissed me off to no end that she wouldn't or couldn't tell me what was going on, I was doing my damnedest to respect her by not pressing her for answers.

After a few minutes, her tears dried up and her breathing evened out. "I'm sorry," she mumbled against my chest.

"You have nothing to be sorry for," I said softly.

"Thank you," she whispered.

"For what?"

She shook her head. "Just, thank you." Then, she raised those honey-colored eyes of hers to mine. With a nod to herself, she reached up with both hands and pulled my head down so she could kiss me. No, she didn't kiss me; she devoured me. One second she was quietly crying against my chest, and the next, she was climbing my body like a tree.

I tried to break the kiss, but she had a firm grasp on me. "Tatum," I mumbled against her lips.

"You want to help me?" she asked and didn't give me a chance to answer. "This is how. I need to let go and forget for a little bit."

Well, who was I to deny a woman in need?

I dropped her to her feet and turned her around, so she was facing the mirror. "Hands on the counter," I said gruffly as I quickly pulled a condom from my wallet and sheathed my cock.

I met her eyes in the mirror. "Is that pussy wet for me?"

To my surprise, she didn't look away or blush when she held my gaze and answered, "Yes."

"Good, stick that ass out and spread those legs wide for me."

I stepped forward and lined my cock up with her entrance. She kept her eyes on mine through the mirror, but something in her gaze made me pause. She wanted a quick, hard fuck, but suddenly, I didn't think that was what she needed.

Stepping back, I gripped her hips and dropped to my knees, making myself eye level with her pretty, pink pussy. Smoothing my hands down her hips, I wrapped them around her thighs while I slowly ran my tongue from front to back one time, relishing in the taste of her.

Sitting back on my heels, I massaged both ass cheeks before pulling them apart and going back in for another slow, torturous swipe of my tongue.

"Trey," she groaned in frustration and earned a slap to her ass.

"Quiet," I barked. "You'll take what I give you."

She used the counter as leverage and pushed back, essentially trying to shove her pussy in my face to get more of what she wanted. I circled her waist with one arm and cradled her head with the other as I yanked her down to the floor. She landed on the cold tile floor with a thump and immediately tried to get up.

Holding her wrists firmly in one hand, I reached with the other to grab the clippers from the countertop. Wrapping the cord around her wrists, I tied her to the toilet seat. It wasn't ideal, but it would have to do.

"That's better," I said and pushed her thighs apart while she glared at me. Fitting my body between her legs, I leaned over her so we were almost nose to nose. "Glare all you want, sugar tits, but you like what I do to you," I said and ran my finger through her wetness. "Don't you?"

Breathing heavily, she kept her eyes, dilated with desire, pinned on me, but she didn't utter a word. I placed my finger against her back entrance and pressed. "If you don't answer me, I'll fuck your tits and leave you tied up in here until I get back from my meeting," I told her and ran my nose up the length of her jaw. Inhaling her intoxicating scent, I pushed two fingers into her wet channel and slipped the tip of one finger into her tight little ass.

Her abdominal muscles flexed and she curled up as best she could. With her teeth bared and sounding like a wild animal, she spat, "You know I do!"

"Yeah, but do you know why you like it?" I chuckled when she basically snarled at me. She was so fucking sexy when she was pissed off. "Letting go and not being in control is something you *need* not something you want."

Pumping my fingers a few times before withdrawing from her body completely, I grinned down at her. "Tell me what you need, baby," I murmured.

She pulled against her restraints as she

writhed on the floor. "Fuck. Me."

"Fuck you where?" I asked and circled her mouth with my finger. "Here?" Moving to her breasts, I cupped them both and pushed them together while circling her nipples with my thumbs. "Or here?"

Releasing her tits, I ran my finger down her torso and slowly pushed it into her pussy. "Maybe here?" I asked with a raised brow. Removing my finger, I moved down lower to her other entrance. "Or here?"

She groaned in frustration. "Trey. Oh, please. I just want you to make me come. Please, please, please," she panted.

"Tell me exactly how you need it, baby, and I'll give it to you." I was as frustrated as she was. My cock was throbbing and all it would take was one good gust of wind for me to explode.

"Fuck," she hissed and bit her bottom lip. "Pinch my nipple with one hand and use the other one to fuck my cunt with your fingers."

I grasped her nipple between my thumb and forefinger and pinched. Hard. "Yes!" she shouted. "Fuck my cunt with your fingers. Fuck it, Trey. Fuck. It."

I grinned and thrust my fingers into her slick

heat. Rotating my hand, I pumped my fingers and tapped against the rough patch of tissue directly behind her clit. "What else do you need, bad girl?"

She was heaving in breaths and her eyes were wild with need. "Suck my other tit and…and… fuck my ass with your finger."

I latched onto her tit and sucked hard, flattening her nipple against the roof of my mouth. At the same time, I dipped a third finger into her pussy before pulling it out and slipping it into her ass.

A high-pitched sound, almost like a dog whistle, came from her as she inhaled sharply. "Oh, fuck. Oh, Trey. Oh, fuck, shit, damn. I'm going to come."

"No!" I snapped and released her tit while removing my fingers from her body. Before she could protest, I slammed my throbbing cock into her and fucked her with everything I had. She was coming before I ever pulled back from the first stroke, screaming my name without a care in the world.

I was so worked up from toying with her that it didn't take long for me to follow her over the edge with my own release.

Knowing Luca would arrive at any moment, Tatum and I made ourselves some lunch and sat at a table in the common room to eat. "Can you eat a little slower? I don't know when he'll arrive or how long it will take, but we need Luca and Cristofano to see you when they leave."

With a mouthful of food, she said, "I am not, nor will I ever be, one of those women who won't eat in front of a man. This body needs fuel to do what it does." She swallowed, nodded to her plate, and took another bite. "This is the first course of what will be a three-course meal. Make that a four-course meal; I forgot about dessert."

I reached down and adjusted my dick. "Fuck, woman. You're going to send me into a serious meeting with a hard-on." She shook her head and chuckled. "That's funny to you?"

"No," she said and wiped her mouth as she continued to laugh. "Sorry. I just remembered that I was going to ask you if that's how you got your road name." At the look of confusion on my face, she continued, "Because of the bat you have in your pants."

I threw my head back and laughed at that.

"Oh, shit, that's good," I managed to say and continued to laugh. When I finally got myself under control, I answered her unasked question. "No, that's not how I got my road name."

Without missing a beat, or a bite of food, she said, "Yeah, I figured that out when I saw Cristofano out cold on the ground and you standing over him with a bat in your hand."

"About that," I started, but had no idea what to say. I wasn't going to apologize or deny who I was, but I hadn't had to answer to anyone since before my mother died.

She waved her hand dismissively. "You don't have to explain yourself to me. I get it, and I'm in no position to be asking you any questions."

An uncomfortable silence fell over us. I opened my mouth to speak but was interrupted by a sharp knock on the front door. Copper entered the room seconds later. "Show time, brothers."

Copper opened the door and gestured for Luca and Piero to come inside. "Gentlemen, follow me to our conference room."

"Gotta go, baby," I said and dropped a kiss on top of Tatum's head before I followed Copper and the other officers to Church.

Tatum reached out and grabbed my hand.

"Are you going to be long?" she asked with a hint of whining in her voice.

"Not sure, baby," I replied and tried not to smile at the clever woman. When I turned around, it was clear her question had drawn Luca's attention—as I'm sure she intended.

Once everyone was seated and the door was closed, Luca asked, "Where is Cristofano?"

"We'll have him brought in after we talk." Without pausing, Copper asked, "Do you know why he came here?"

Luca clasped his hands on the table and studied Copper for several long beats. "He has been searching for someone. I presume something in his search led him here, but I do not know that for certain."

"Who is he searching for?" Copper asked.

"His fiancée, Adrianna. She disappeared under mysterious circumstances several months ago. He's been searching for her ever since," Luca explained.

"I see. Well, for whatever reason, Cristofano showed up at our clubhouse around one o'clock in the morning, drove his car through our gate, and forced his way inside because he thought we had her."

Luca blinked slowly but otherwise didn't react to Copper's words. "I will cover the cost of any damage he caused to your property."

Copper nodded in agreement. "We aren't in the business of selling women, Luca. Never have been and never will be. I know a lot of clubs get a bad rap—it comes with the territory—but we're not a one-percent club. If a woman came to us for help, we'd help her; we wouldn't hold her here against her will, and we damn sure don't kidnap people."

"Technically, you are currently kidnapping my associate," Luca countered.

"Women. We don't kidnap women," Copper snapped. "Innocent women. We don't kidnap innocent women."

The corner of Luca's mouth slightly curved upward for a brief moment. "Understood. I do apologize for his behavior, and I can assure you, he will not bother you again."

"Batta, go get Cristofano."

I walked out to the shed where Coal and Grant were playing a game of cards while Cristofano appeared to be sleeping. "You two are free to go," I announced.

Coal threw his cards on the table and headed

for the door. "Thank fuck."

I undid Cristofano's restraints and frog-marched him to Church. Surprisingly, he remained silent the entire time. I was prepared for more verbal threats and possibly a physical struggle, but he'd either worn himself out or knew he was about to face his unhappy boss.

We entered the room as Copper was saying, "…had my guy look him over, and he has a bit of a concussion, but he'll be fine."

Luca's eyes immediately went to Cristofano and he scowled. Before any of us could react, Luca had a gun in his hand aimed at Cristofano's head. "Apologize."

I stepped out of the line of fire as Cristofano fell to his knees. He dropped his head. "Please forgive me."

"Just so you're aware, we have some type of federal agent sitting in the common room," Copper interjected.

Luca nodded once. "Yes, I'm aware of Tatum Cross's presence, though I thank you for the warning."

I was taken aback by his response. How in the hell did he know Tatum?

With his gun still trained on Cristofano, Luca

continued, "You will pay for any and all damage to their property, and you will stay away. If that's going to be a problem for you, I'll make sure it isn't right this very second."

"It won't be a problem, boss," Cristofano vowed. I didn't know the man, but judging by his body language and the tone of his voice, I believed him.

Luca slipped his gun into the shoulder holster hidden under his suit jacket and turned to Copper. "Are you satisfied with our offered amends?"

Copper leaned back in his chair and rubbed his chin as if he was mulling it over. "Do I have your word that this won't be an issue for us in the future?"

And there it was. Asking a man like Luca to give his word was the equivalent of asking him to sign it in blood.

"You have my word," Luca vowed.

"Well then, I don't believe we have anything further to discuss."

"If you'll show Piero to Cristofano's car, Cristofano will be riding with me," Luca announced as he got to his feet.

"Of course," Copper agreed and looked to

me. I gave a brief, nonchalant shake of my head. Copper cleared his throat. "His car suffered damage as a result of driving through our gate. I'm sure you understand."

"His car's condition is of no concern to me," Luca replied instantly.

Copper nodded. "Judge will pull his car around front."

"Very well," Luca replied and got to his feet. "Again, I sincerely apologize for my associate's behavior. I truly appreciate your understanding in this matter."

Copper also stood and extended his hand. "You helped us out a few months ago. We were just returning the favor."

After shaking Copper's hand, Luca moved toward the door. "Thank you, again." He then directed his attention to Cristofano, who was still kneeling on the floor. "Get up and get in my car. You can use the ride home to convince me not to shoot you once we get there."

Cristofano obeyed Luca's command and silently followed him outside while Piero fell in line behind them. Judge was waiting out front and handed Cristofano's keys to Piero. They didn't linger, and within a few moments, they were gone.

20

TATUM

While the men were meeting with Luca, I sat in the common room staring at the television. I couldn't have told you what was on the screen because my mind was consumed with thoughts of Josie. My job had been to protect her, but now that she was in a different location, I wondered what Luke was going to do with me. I didn't see a need for me to stay in Devil Springs without Josie.

"You okay?" Heidi asked as she placed a tray with chips and salsa and two drinks on the table.

"Oh, yeah, I'm good," I said distractedly.

"Mind if I join you?" she asked.

I pushed the chair out with my foot. "Be my

guest." I wasn't feeling exceptionally social, but I welcomed the distraction.

"So, how'd you meet Batta?"

"We got shot together," I said simply.

"What?" she gasped.

"Sorry, I don't have a filter. Actually, I'm not really sorry. It is what it is."

She waved her hand dismissively. "I hang around an MC; I'm used to it. I just didn't realize you were the woman that helped them."

I nodded. "Yeah, I was one of them. My sister, Josie, helped Bronze while I helped Batta."

"Thank you," she said softly. "For helping them."

I studied her for a few moments while she focused on the tortilla chip she was twirling with her fingers. "Oh," I said as it dawned on me. "You must be Bronze's girlfriend."

She looked up and shook her head. "No, I'm not his, or anyone's, girlfriend," she said solemnly.

"I see," I said, and I did. She was clearly in love with Bronze, and judging by her response, he had no idea. I had no interest in delving into that conversation, so I did us both a solid and changed the subject. "You want to have some fun?"

"Uh, that depends on what you mean by fun," she said hesitantly.

I grinned. "I thought we could play a harmless, little prank on one or two of the guys."

"Oh, hell yes. What do you have in mind?"

After I explained, we went to the kitchen and gathered our supplies. Then, we snuck down the hall to Bronze's room. After we finished in his room, I opened the door to head to Batta's room and saw Judge walking down the hall. "Shit. I think their meeting's over, and I'm supposed to be in the common room. We'll have to get Batta later."

She stashed our supplies in the kitchen and joined me at the table in the common room. "It's probably just as well. Once one of them figured it out, they'd all check to make sure they hadn't been pranked, too."

"Very true," I agreed and shoved a chip into my mouth.

"I hope I'm here when it happens," she whispered.

I laughed. "Yeah, me too."

When we heard the men coming down the hall, I tried to appear relaxed as I engaged Heidi in conversation. “So, how long have you been coming to the clubhouse?”

She shrugged. “A couple of years, I guess. My friend wanted to go to one of their parties and asked me to come with her. We had a lot of fun, and some of the guys invited us to the next party. We kept coming back, and somewhere along the way, they asked us to help out around the club with cleaning and bartending.”

“Who’s your friend?”

“Paige.”

“Oh, I don’t think I’ve met her.”

“You haven’t. She stopped coming around the club after Bronze and Batta got hurt. Then, about two weeks ago, she moved away,” she said sadly.

“Did she move far away?” I asked.

Heidi shrugged again. “I don’t know. She stopped talking to me. I only knew she moved because I ran into her mother at the grocery store.”

“Did you two have a fight or something?”

“No, but a while back, the clubhouse was attacked, and we got hurt, but we were both convinced it was a one-time thing. When Bronze and Batta were attacked, I think it scared her more than she was willing to admit." She paused for a moment and picked up another chip to twirl. "I get where she's coming from, but I wish she would've talked to me about it. We've been best friends for seven years. I wouldn't have tried to talk her out of moving away if that's what she wanted."

"One thing I can tell you for certain is that people show their true colors during stressful situations. Scared or not, there's no excuse for the way she treated you. You deserved more than that from her. It's never okay for anyone to treat you like crap, especially the ones who claim to love you. Remember that."

"How old are you?" she asked.

Her question caught me off guard, but I didn't have a problem answering her. "Twenty-nine. Why do you ask?"

She smiled shyly. "You look young, but it seems like you have a lot of wisdom. Those two don't usually go hand in hand."

I laughed. "You're right about that."

I felt a presence behind me before a large hand landed on my shoulder. "What're you girls doing?" Trey asked.

"Sewing a quilt," I deadpanned.

"Smart-ass," he grumbled and pulled out a chair.

"Did your guests leave?" I asked.

"Sure did," he said and popped a chip into his mouth.

Heidi pushed back from the table. "Well, I guess I better get back to work. Nice chatting with you."

I moved to get up as well, but Trey stopped me. "Where're you going?"

"Back to my room. I need to call Luke."

"All right," he said and reached out to squeeze my ass. "Come find me when you're finished."

"Will do."

Once in my room, I closed the door and locked it. Then, as an added precaution, I went into the bathroom and turned on the shower before I dialed Luke's number.

"Hello, Tatum. What can I do for you this afternoon?" he asked jovially.

"Shut it, old man. You know why I'm calling."

"How did it go?"

"Good? I mean, there was no bloodshed. They were here for about thirty minutes or so before they left."

"Did they see you?"

"I don't know if Cristofano did, but Luca and Piero did. I made sure of it."

"Good. Now that we don't have to worry about Cristofano blowing our entire operation, we can focus our attention elsewhere and hopefully get this wrapped up soon."

"About that. Do I need to stay in Devil Springs now that Josie isn't here?" I asked.

"Yes, you do. And before you start arguing, listen to me. We have to stick with our cover story. I promise, Tatum, we are doing everything we can to end this, but you, of all people, know that these things take time," he explained. And damn it, he was right.

"Yeah," I sighed. "I know."

"Since Josie is going to remain at the new location for the time being, you can return to the safe house and resume your regular work schedule at the store," he told me.

"I'm not doing anything until I have a new car."

Luke laughed. "Good news. Since it turned out to be Cristofano following you, you can have the truck back. I'll have someone drop it off at the clubhouse and pick up the minivan."

"I suppose I hate you a little less right now."

"Gotta go. We'll talk soon," he said abruptly and ended the call.

Well, shit. As much as I bitched and moaned about being at the clubhouse, I wasn't exactly looking forward to leaving. One thing was for sure though, if I was going back to the safe house, I was moving my ass into the main house. There was a huge bathtub in the master bedroom that was calling my name.

Exhaling slowly, I turned off the shower and went back into the bedroom to start packing my things. It was then that I realized we'd left all of Josie's belongings behind in our rush to get out of the clubhouse. I packed her stuff separately and sent a text to Luke. I told him I would put her bag in the minivan so he could make sure it got to her.

On my way back inside from putting Josie's things in the van, I heard a string of expletives come from Bronze's room. I slapped a hand over my mouth and stepped inside my room, leaving the door wide open so I wouldn't miss any of the show.

Bronze came out of his bedroom clad only in a pair of boxer briefs with one arm held straight in the air. "Seriously?" he bellowed, pointing to his armpit as he stomped down the hall. "Which one of you fuckers did this?"

"Did what?" Trey asked.

"This?" Bronze stressed and pointed again.

"The fuck is with you and your armpit, man? That shit looks nasty."

"It feels nasty!" he said indignantly. "And it smells like pie! Why does my pit smell like pie?"

Trey sniffed the air, then threw his head back and laughed. "Someone replaced your deodorant with cream cheese!" Bronze scowled and scooped a handful of the creamy gunk from his armpit and smeared it on Trey's head. "You motherfucker," Trey growled and tackled him to the ground.

Bronze landed hard, and Trey took the opportunity to use Bronze's clean armpit to wipe the cream cheese from his head.

"What the fuck is going on out here?" Copper roared.

Bronze and Trey froze for all of one second before they pointed at each other and said, "He started it."

"I did not," they both said at the same time.

Copper shook his head at the two of them

and turned on his heels, disappearing down the hallway.

And I got the whole thing on video.

When both men got to their feet, I slipped back into my room and closed the door, hoping I hadn't been seen. A few minutes later, Trey opened the door without knocking and walked inside. He glanced around the room and narrowed his eyes. "Going somewhere?"

"Yep. Apparently, I'm being released early for good behavior."

He snorted. "Yeah, right. What's really going on?"

I shrugged. "Nothing's going on. Luke said I could go home."

"Home?" he croaked.

"Yes," I nodded. "I need to get back to work. That store isn't going to get itself ready for opening. And now that Josie's gone, I'm going to have to bust my ass to have things ready on time," I explained.

"You're staying in Devil Springs?" he asked.

"Yes," I said slowly. "We're opening a bookstore next to your gym, remember?"

"When are you leaving?" he asked and stepped closer to me.

"As soon as my truck is delivered. I refuse to go anywhere in that minivan if I don't have to," I said seriously.

He'd slowly closed the distance between us and was standing directly in front of me. He leaned forward and pressed his mouth to my neck, gently nipping at my skin. "Come shower with me," he said as he kissed his way up to my ear. "Unless you want me to tell Bronze you're the one who put cream cheese in his deodorant."

"What?" I asked, trying to sound surprised.

"Don't even try it, woman. I saw you and Heidi on the surveillance cameras."

Shit. I had forgotten about those. "You gonna rat me out?"

"Not if you take a shower with me," he said slyly.

"Okay, big guy, a shower it is."

21

BATTA

I lasted all of five hours before I caved, and I didn't give the first fuck what anybody thought about it. Tatum had gone back to her place as planned, and I didn't like it one bit. I knew she couldn't tell me anything, and I knew she could handle herself, but that didn't stop me from worrying about her. The leftover anger from her secrets and my growing concern for her had me so worked up that I was ready to fuck her three ways from Sunday the moment I saw her.

My worry increased ten-fold when I knocked on the little red door, and no one answered. "Tatum," I called out as I moved to peek through one of the windows.

"You'd make a shitty spy," Tatum said from behind me, effectively scaring the fuck out of me.

I straightened and whirled around to see her standing with her arms crossed over her chest and a smug look on her face. "Most people just answer the door."

"I would have if you'd have knocked on that door," she said and pointed to the back door leading into the main house.

"Why'd you decide to move?"

"This one has a bigger bathtub," she said flatly. "What are you doing here?"

I shrugged. "I was in the neighborhood." I couldn't put my finger on it, but something seemed off. She wasn't throwing out sarcastic comments or doing something kooky like she usually was.

"You were worried about me," she said knowingly.

I looked down at my feet and rubbed the toe of my boot into the ground. "I know you can handle yourself, but fuck, Tatum, how could I not be worried about you?"

"Aw, the big, grumpy biker has feelings," she taunted.

I turned her by her shoulders and smacked her ass. "Get your punk ass inside."

She huffed dramatically. "Fine."

I followed her through the back door into the kitchen. My mouth dropped open when I took in the room. "Who in the hell lives here?"

"I do," she deadpanned.

"You did this shit?" I asked incredulously. There were mushrooms everywhere—mushroom handles on the cabinets and doors, mushroom wallpaper, a mushroom table and chairs. Even the ceiling had striations making it look like the underside of a mushroom cap.

"Yep," she said and managed to hold a straight face for about fifteen seconds before she burst into a fit of laughter. "Damn it! I wanted to show you the other rooms before I cracked."

"There's more?"

She laughed even harder. "You have no idea. Follow me." She led me down a normal looking hallway and stopped in front of a closed door. She flung the door open and made a grand gesture with her arms. "I give you…The Doll Room."

I took two steps into the room and immediately backed out after one glance. The walls were lined with cabinets filled with creepy-ass porcelain dolls of all shapes and sizes. Pulling the door closed, I turned to Tatum, "Does this door lock?"

She snorted and shook her head. "No, but I sure as fuck wish it did." She laughed again. "I promise, the next room isn't that bad."

Reluctantly, I followed her back to the kitchen. When she opened a door and started walking down a flight of stairs that I assumed led to a basement, I stopped and braced my arms on the door frame. "Sorry, babe, but this has got Hell-Fucking-No written all over it."

She turned around and arched an eyebrow. "Scared?"

"No, sugar tits. Not scared. Smart."

She sighed and started making her way back upstairs. "Fine, then. No sex dungeon for you," she mumbled.

"Wait. What did you say?" I asked and pulled her against me.

"There's a kinky sex dungeon in the basement. I thought it might interest you," she said huskily.

"You serious?"

"Come see for yourself."

I studied her face but couldn't tell if she was

fucking with me or not. She patiently waited for me to make my decision. I nodded my head toward the stairs. "Let's see this kinky sex dungeon."

She led the way and stopped in front of a closed door. Turning to face me, she chewed on her lower lip. "It's not really a sex dungeon," she confessed and opened the door. "It's a kick-ass wine cellar."

I stepped inside and looked around. "Why didn't you just say that?"

She shrugged. "I didn't think you'd be interested."

My forehead wrinkled in confusion while I studied her. Something was off, but I couldn't put my finger on it. "What aren't you telling me?"

"Nothing," she said and shrugged again. "Have a look around."

Appeasing her, I slowly walked around the cellar while she silently watched me. Truthfully, I'd never been in a wine cellar before; it was much larger than I expected.

I stopped when I came to a section of wine bottles on the back wall. Noting the faint cut out around the entire case, I glanced at Tatum over my shoulder. "Something back here?"

"I can't say that there is," she answered flatly.

That's when it finally clicked—she was trying to tell me something without actually telling me.

"Huh, guess it's just a crack in the foundation. You should probably have that checked," I suggested and continued making my way around the cellar.

The name on a bottle of wine caught my eye. *Hustle.* I picked it up to get a better look. Tatum came up from behind me and took the bottle from my hands. "This is a damn good wine. Let's take this bottle upstairs so you can try it."

"You can do that?" I asked. I knew the house didn't belong to her, so I assumed the wine didn't belong to her either.

She laughed. "Normally, no, but I have a few cases of my own wine down here, and that's one of them."

"I didn't peg you for a wine drinker."

Grabbing my hand, she pulled me from the room and headed upstairs. "Wait until you try it."

"This sounds like something the Old Ladies would like. Where'd you find it?"

"I was on an assignment and found it at Elevation 966, a locally owned winery in Greenville, South Carolina."

In the land of mushrooms, she uncorked the bottle and poured us each a glass. I brought the glass to my lips and emptied its contents in two swallows. "That is good."

When I looked up, Tatum was staring at me as she slowly swirled her glass. "Did you even taste it?"

I smacked my lips together. "Yes?"

"It's not beer, Trey. You're supposed to sip it, slowly, so you can savor the flavor."

I grinned and took the glass from her hand. Stepping forward, I pulled her against me. "I'd rather savor your flavor," I said and ran my nose along her jawline.

"I'll get the wine. You grab the glasses," she said and headed for the stairs.

I did as she asked and followed her upstairs to a bathroom that was bigger than most bedrooms, and the bathtub was about the size of a double bed.

"I was planning on taking a long soak in the tub. Care to join me?" she asked.

"Are you going to fill it up with girly smelling bubbles?" I asked.

She grinned. "What if I said yes?"

I dropped into a chair situated in the corner

of the bathroom. “Then, I’d sit right here and watch.”

She sighed dramatically. “Fine. I won’t put any ‘girly smelling bubbles’ in it.” Not waiting for my reply, she stripped off her clothes and stepped into the steamy water.

Damn. The woman’s body was a masterpiece. Flawless skin, except for a handful of scars. Toned muscles. A nice, firm ass. And her tits were the most perfect pair to ever grace the earth. I palmed my dick and groaned in appreciation.

“You know, if you got in here with me, I could help you with that.”

She didn’t need to tell me twice. Quickly shucking my clothes, I stepped closer to the tub. Before I could step in, she stopped me by wrapping her lips around my hard cock.

I groaned and tightly gripped her hair. “I’m not a gentle man,” I warned.

“Mmmhmm,” she hummed and proceeded to slide her lips up and down my cock in a slow and teasing manner.

I yanked her head back by her hair and tilted her face so her eyes could meet mine. “Are you going to suck my dick or am I going to make you?”

Perched on her knees with her legs spread open and droplets of water running over her breasts, she grinned at me mischievously. "Make me."

"Fuck, yes," I breathed and thrust my length between her plump lips. Using her hair to hold her head steady, I fucked her mouth with no shame, and she took everything I gave her.

When I looked down, she had one hand between her legs while the other toyed with her right nipple. I pushed to the back of her throat and held myself there. "You like to be mouth fucked, sugar tits?"

She met my eyes and nodded her head as best she could while moaning around me.

I pulled out and gave her a moment to catch her breath before I shoved my cock back into her mouth. "That pussy is mine. I make it come," I growled, each word punctuated with a thrust. "Not. You," I declared and held her against me when my cock hit the back of her throat on the last word.

She blinked up at me with watery eyes and swallowed. Swallowed. Then, she pulled some kind of voodoo hoodoo out of nowhere and somehow massaged my dick with the walls of her throat.

There was nothing I could do to stop it, to warn her. The come shot out of my dick so fast and hard it almost hurt. I released her hair and tried to push her away, but she dug her nails into my ass cheeks and held on tight, swallowing every bit of my release.

When I was finished, she pulled back and looked up at me while I stumbled back and collapsed into the chair.

I closed my eyes and took a minute to catch my breath. Holy. Shit. That was by far the most intense orgasm I'd ever experienced. Once I had myself somewhat composed, I opened my eyes to see Tatum staring at me with her tits propped on the edge of the tub. She winked, "Sucked you dry, didn't I?"

I smirked and stalked to the tub. "My turn."

22

TATUM

"Luke, what in the hell are we doing?" I shouted into the phone. Two weeks had passed since I moved Josie to another location, and absolutely nothing had happened.

During the week, I went to the store as instructed, though I spent most of my time researching anything and everything I could think of related to Josie's case instead of actually getting the store ready to open. I was tired of waiting for my team to come through with something helpful, but despite my efforts, I hadn't found anything useful either.

Luke sighed. "We're doing our jobs, Tatum. Investigations of this magnitude can take months, sometimes years. I'm doing everything in my power to speed things up, but there's only so much I can do without completely blowing the case."

"Fine," I huffed in annoyance and disconnected the call.

There was only so much he could do, but there had to be something more I could do, especially since I was no longer in charge of protecting Josie.

It hit me all of a sudden, and I wanted to scream at myself for not thinking of it sooner. Instead of beating around the bush, I was going to go straight to the source, or one of the sources.

Without giving it a second thought, I climbed into my truck and headed for the man I hoped would have some answers for me.

DESPITE THE NERVES CHURNING IN MY GUT, I forced myself to appear calm and confident on the outside. Truthfully, there was a fifty-fifty chance I might have my head blown off for even showing up on the property.

"Miss Cross, right this way, please," an older man said by way of greeting.

"Sorry, Jeeves, that's not happening until I know where you're taking me."

"I do apologize, Miss Cross. I assumed you're here to speak with the man of the house. His office is right down the hall."

"You assumed correctly. Carry on," I said and gestured with my hands for him to continue.

When we reached a heavily lacquered wooden door at the end of the hallway, he sharply knocked one time before cracking the door open and saying, "Miss Cross is here to see you, sir."

"Thank you, Donovan. Send her in."

Donovan stepped to the side and ushered me into the room that suddenly felt much smaller than it actually was. Sitting in a high-back leather office chair dressed from head-to-toe in a custom-tailored three-piece suit with his keen eyes staring straight at me was Luca Peccati.

"Miss Cross, to what do I owe the pleasure of your unexpected visit?"

I stepped closer to his desk but didn't take a seat. Keeping my back straight and meeting his eyes, I said, "I need your help."

I expected him to laugh in my face or kick me

out of his house. Instead, he clasped his hands together, leaned forward, and uttered the one name I was hoping to hear. "Is this about Sheldon Morgan?"

I swallowed audibly and nodded. "Yes, it is."

"And what makes you think I can help? You have access to resources that are far superior to mine."

"All the technology in the world won't grant me the connections you have."

His lips curled in disgust. "I do not have connections to Sheldon Morgan."

I took a seat in one of the chairs in front of his desk and crossed my arms over my chest. "Yes, you do. Cristofano."

"Cristofano despises Sheldon".

"And that's what I came for. I need to know why."

Luca sighed and leaned back in his chair. "There are only two reasons that cause men to hate each other—a woman or money."

I waited for him to continue. When he didn't, I asked, "Which one is it?"

"Both."

I pinched the bridge of my nose. I was not in the mood to coax information from him bit by bit. "Will you please just tell me what happened?"

He narrowed his eyes and tilted his head to the side. "How would sharing their personal story with you be beneficial for me?"

I slapped my palms on my thighs and got to my feet. "Fuck this shit! I don't have time for ass kissing and bullshit games. Thank you for your time, but I'll figure out something else."

"Sit down, Tatum," he ordered in a calm yet firm tone.

I glared at him. "Say please."

He pulled a handgun from the pocket of his suit jacket and placed it on his desk. "I will not tolerate disrespect from anyone, especially not in my own damn office. Now, sit. Down."

I didn't sit. Instead, I pulled my own gun from its holster and pointed it toward the floor. "I don't tolerate disrespect either, Mr. Peccati. Now, if we're finished with the pissing contest, I have business to tend to."

He removed something from a drawer and stood. He held up the small, black device for me to see. "May I?"

I smirked and held my arms out to either side. "Go right ahead." He nodded and slowly moved the device up and down my body, checking to see if I had any hidden cameras or listening devices.

When he finished, he smiled. "Not even a cell phone. I'm impressed, Miss Cross."

"Really, Mr. Peccati? I'm not an idiot," I said and rubbed my chest. "I'm slightly offended you think so little of me."

"You don't give a single fuck what I think of you, and we both know it. Now, have a seat, and we'll continue our conversation."

I bit down on the inside of my cheek to keep the sarcastic remark from leaving my lips as I resentfully followed his command.

He returned to his seat behind his desk and took his time making himself comfortable. When he reached into another drawer, I wanted to scream at him to hurry up but managed to contain myself. Placing two glasses on the desk, he poured an amber liquid into each and pushed one in my direction.

I didn't want the drink, but I learned early on how to follow social cues and this was one I had to go along with in order to get what I wanted. So, I brought the glass to my lips and took a small sip, ignoring the burn as it made its way down to my stomach.

After watching me, Luca took a sip from his glass and finally started to talk. "Adrianna is the daughter of the well-known media mogul Simon Barrington."

My head shot up at his words. "What?" I breathed.

He nodded and continued, "Five years ago, Simon Barrington promised Adrianna's hand to Nolan Morgan's son Sheldon. During her last year of college, she was informed of her upcoming nuptials when she came home for winter break. Adrianna had a boyfriend at school and had no intention of marrying Sheldon. When she returned to school, she told her boyfriend about her father's plans. I'll spare you the details of how it was done, but one day, she seemingly vanished."

"And by 'vanished,' you mean she ran off with Cristofano?"

"Infer as you wish."

I sat quietly for a few minutes and processed the new information while Luca slowly sipped his drink. "What was the reason behind the marriage?" I asked.

"Every arranged marriage has the same reason behind it—an increase in power."

"How would a marriage between Adrianna and Sheldon result in an increase in power for either family?"

Luca shook his head. "I don't know the answer to that."

"If you had to take an educated guess, what would it be?" I asked, pushing for more.

He reached into his desk and produced a folder. Pushing it to the edge closest to me, he said, "You cannot take that, but you may look at it while you're here."

It was all I could do to refrain from snatching it from the desk like a greedy child. Leaning forward, I picked up the folder and studied the contents. I carefully read each page. When I reached the bottom of the third page, Luca pointed out, "The sixth and seventh pages should be of interest to you."

Flipping to the sixth page, I began to read, and my jaw dropped open.

Simon Barrington owned a private island in the Caribbean.

Nolan Morgan owned two extremely large yachts—one was kept in Cape Town, South Africa, and the other was kept in Rio de Janeiro, Brazil.

"With the information you already know, it shouldn't be difficult to put the pieces together," Luca suggested.

"Holy shit," I breathed. And then something else suddenly dawned on me. "What am I going to owe you for this?"

Luca threw his head back and laughed. "Oh, Miss Cross, that's cute."

When I continued to stare at him, waiting for him to give me the real answer, he finally gave in. "Other than not revealing me as your source, just put a stop to it. That's all I ask."

"I will, or I'll die trying," I vowed. "And thank you."

"You're welcome. Should I expect any other visitors today? Perhaps from your boss or your biker man?"

I jumped to my feet and placed the folder on his desk. "Shit! I've got to go." With that, I ran out of Luca Peccati's house like my ass was on fire. Because I had a feeling it would be if I didn't get back to Devil Springs before Trey realized I wasn't at the store.

My steps faltered. I'd never cared what anyone thought about my actions—not my family nor my boss, and certainly not a man. But I suddenly realized that I didn't want him to be worried, like I knew he would be. And just as quickly, I pushed the thought to the back of my mind. I'd have to comb through my feeling for the big, grumpy biker later.

23

BATTA

After helping Judge install a security system at a new client's house, I stopped by the gym to hang out with Coal and Savior before squeezing in a light workout while I waited for Tatum to finish up at the shop. She usually called it a day around five o'clock, and since she made it perfectly clear that I was not to disturb her while she was working, I waited for her to let me know when she was finished for the day.

When I hadn't heard from her by six o'clock, I started to get worried. "Have you seen Tatum today?" I asked Savior.

"No, but we don't usually see her. Is something wrong?"

I shook my head. "Nah, she probably got busy

and lost track of time." Savior gave me an incredulous look but didn't comment. I couldn't blame him; I didn't believe what I'd just said either.

"I'm gonna go see what she's up to. I'll catch ya later, man," I said as I headed out the back door.

I reached for the door and twisted the knob, pleased to find it locked. "Tatum!" I called as I knocked on the back door. An uneasy feeling started to form in the pit of my stomach. "Tatum!" I yelled again.

Slowly, I turned around and cursed when I realized her truck wasn't parked in its usual spot. Just as I reached the back door to the gym, her door swung open and there stood Tatum, heaving in breath after breath. "Sorry! I was in the backroom stacking boxes."

I grimaced. "I wish you'd let me help you with that."

"So you've said. Many times."

"You ready to go?" I asked.

She glanced at her phone and gasped. "I didn't realize it was so late. Yeah, let me grab my keys and lock up."

"Where's your truck?" I asked.

"Oh, when I came back from picking up lunch, a delivery truck was blocking the spaces in the back, so I parked out front."

I walked through the gym and waited for her in front of her store. When she came out, she was holding her laptop and a notebook in her arms, making it difficult for her to lock the door.

"Would you like some help?" I asked and reached for the computer.

She tightened her hold on it and shook her keys at me. "Would you lock the door for me?"

"Sure," I said and plucked the keys from her fingers. Once the door was secured, I started to walk her to her truck, but she stopped me.

"Will this fit in your saddlebags?" she asked and held up her computer. "I'd really like to go for a ride before going home."

"You okay?"

"Yep," she said quickly. Then, her shoulders sagged, and she sighed. "Maybe not. I've had a lot on my mind today."

I took the items from her hands and carefully placed them in my saddlebags. She climbed on right behind me and snuggled close to my back. "Hold on tight, baby, and let the wind take it all away."

We rode for over an hour before she asked me to take her home. I wasn't keen on the idea of letting her spend the rest of the evening alone, but I knew she'd argue if I said as much. So, I kept my mouth shut and drove us to the clubhouse. Regardless of who was there, Friday nights at the clubhouse were always fun.

"What are we doing here?" she asked when I shut off the engine.

"We're going inside to have some fun," I said and walked to the front door before she had a chance to protest.

As expected, she followed along behind me. "Tatum!" River shouted from across the room as she waved her hand in the air.

Tatum grinned. "Oh yes, this was a great idea." However, her grin disappeared when Kennedy came around the corner and took a seat beside River.

I slid my arm around Tatum's waist and pulled her close to my side. "She's not a threat to you, and you know it."

"Yes, but if she doesn't keep her tits off of your arm, I will most certainly be a threat to her."

I couldn't hold back my laugh. "What?"

Tatum rolled her eyes and scoffed. Then, she

proceeded to demonstrate exactly what she meant by thrusting her tits on either side of my arm. "Is she only capable of talking to you from the side?"

"I doubt she even realizes she's doing it, but I'll make sure to stay in front of her during any conversations," I promised.

"You do that," she snapped.

"Do you want to leave?" I asked.

"No, I want her to leave," she said flatly.

I sighed. "She's River's friend and coworker. If you'd give her a chance, you'd see that she's a nice person."

"Please, continue to explain to me how I should be friends with your ex-girlfriend."

Wrapping my hand around her neck, I pulled her close to me and kissed the skin beneath her ear. "You need me to fuck that bad attitude out of you?"

Kissing down her neck, I lightly bit the sensitive spot where her neck and shoulder met. "Maybe making your cunt come a few times will put a smile on your face."

Using my other hand to grab a handful of her firm ass, I pressed her against my hard dick. "Say the word, baby, and I'll fuck you so hard you won't be able to walk tomorrow."

She groaned and climbed my body like a tree, wrapping her legs around my waist. Digging her fingers into my short hair, she held on and buried her face in my neck. “Yes, please.”

24

TATUM

Trey wasn't exaggerating. I could barely walk when I snuck out of bed to call Luke. He was going to be furious with me, but I didn't have the time or patience to drop hints and let him figure it out on his own.

"Johnson," he answered sleepily.

"Cross," I snapped. "Get up. I have information."

Material rustled in the background, followed by the unmistakable sound of flowing urine. "Are you seriously pissing right now?"

"Fuck. I thought I hit mute. Give me a second."

The line was filled with dead air as I assumed he finished his morning ablutions. When he finally came back on the line, I was well and truly irritated.

"All right, Cross, what's so important?"

"Don't be mad. Well, don't be too mad."

"What did you do?" he growled.

Clearing my throat, I gave it to him straight. "I went to speak with Luca Peccati."

"You did what?" he roared.

"I won't apologize for it. He had what we needed."

"You're telling me you walked into Luca Peccati's house, and he just handed over the information we've been trying to get our hands on for months? At what cost, Tatum?"

"If you'll shut up for two seconds, I'll tell you exactly what happened."

"By all means, go right ahead."

While I filled him in on my visit with Luca Peccati, he huffed and puffed the entire time, but he didn't utter a single word when I finished. Pulling the phone away from my ear, I glanced at the screen to make sure the call was still connected.

"Luke?" I asked.

"I'm here. Just…hold on. I'm processing."

As I had hoped, he didn't sound as pissed as

he previously did once he heard what I had to say.

"I'm looking through everything right now. Simon has one daughter named Clarise, not Adrianna. We don't have any record of any property belonging to Simon Barrington in or around the Caribbean."

"It's not in his name. Are you new?" I snapped.

"Connect the dots, Tatum."

"Clarise Barrington was supposed to marry Nolan Sheldon Morgan II. Run the name Clarise Morgan."

I waited quietly while listening to the keyboard clicking in the background. "And there it is," he almost whispered.

"The yachts are registered to her, too. I didn't have time to run a full check, but I found a few other properties under her name; all are on the coast, too."

"Listen, Tatum, while you did come up with some very useful information, you cannot, absolutely cannot, go off on your own and do shit like this again. Understood?"

"I mean, yeah, I hear you and all, but I won't make a promise unless I'm one-hundred-percent sure I can keep it."

"Damn it, Tatum."

"Sorry, not sorry, boss man," I retorted.

"I would've rather you lied to me," he grumbled.

"I do enough lying because of this job as it is. I won't add more to the pile." It was the one thing I hated about my job—the constant lying, especially when we were undercover.

He sighed. "I know how you feel about that, but it is a necessity."

"Blah, blah, blah. Spare me the pep talk and get busy with the info I just handed you. I'm beyond ready for this to be over."

"Me too, but the original plan hasn't changed. This information will help, tremendously, but we're going to have to catch them in the act if we want to be absolutely certain they can't get out of it."

"Well, then, that's what we'll do."

"Tatum—" he started, but I ended the call before he could start lecturing me. I knew the importance of handling an investigation properly, especially when high-profile, wealthy suspects were involved. One wrong move and the whole case would be blown.

25

TATUM

As soon as the clock struck five o'clock, I packed up my shit and flew out the door. As much as I complained about it in the beginning, I really did like setting up the bookstore, but it was much more fun when Josie was around. I knew Trey was helping out at the bar his club owned, so I decided to pop into the gym for a workout before heading back to the safe house.

When I walked through the front doors, Bronze was standing in front of a little girl looking like a deer in headlights. I started to laugh, which drew his attention to me. "Tay!" he shouted, and the relief in his voice was evident.

"Yes, broody biker?"

"Uh," he shifted uncomfortably. "This is Jenna," he said and gestured to the little girl. "She's eight years old and is here for her self-defense class."

"Okay…"

He leaned closer and quickly whispered, "We don't have a self-defense class. We don't have any classes."

I smirked and crossed my arms over my chest. "You're going to have to ask."

To my surprise, he didn't hesitate. "Will you help me teach her some self-defense moves?"

"Say please."

"Don't push it," he grumbled.

I reached out to pat his chest but remembered his wound at the last second and placed my hand on his shoulder. "Just checking to make sure you still had your balls."

"Of course I do," he snorted and started to grab his crotch but stopped when I jerked my head to Jenna.

"So, you're just scared of kids? Interesting," I mused. He opened his mouth to argue, but I didn't give him the opportunity. "Get one of your employees and show me where an empty room is."

"Grant!" Bronze shouted. "Need you to get suited up downstairs."

"Hi, Jenna. I'm Tay. Are you ready to learn how to kick some butt?"

"Yes, ma'am," she said quietly, never making eye contact with me.

I dropped to a squat in front of her. "Jenna," I said softly. "Look at me." When she did, I smiled and tried to make her feel more comfortable. "This is going to be fun. We're going to go downstairs, and I'm going to show you how to defend yourself if you ever need to. I'll go first, okay?"

She finally met my eyes, and my heart melted at the worry filling hers. "Okay," she whispered.

I knew, just from my brief interaction with her, something had happened to her, and I was going to make damn sure she could prevent anything else from happening.

"Bronze, would it be possible for Riley to join our class?" I asked quietly, but little ears still heard me.

"Mommy told me Riley would be here," Jenna mumbled.

Right on cue, Savior burst through the front doors with Riley in his arms. "Sorry we're late! I thought it was scheduled for tomorrow night." He paused and glanced around. "Where's Batta?"

"Working security for Precious Metals," Bronze said.

Savior chuckled and placed Riley on her feet. "I think Jenna's mom got the date wrong, not us. Batta was supposed to show them self-defense moves."

"May I ask why a seven-year-old and eight-year-old need to be taught self-defense by an MC enforcer?"

Savior sighed. "There's an older girl in the neighborhood who we think is bullying the younger kids. It's not your typical schoolyard bullying; it's hard to put into words how she does it. It's like she manipulates them into doing things that she knows they shouldn't do. We don't let Riley play with her, but she still shows up at the playground and is all over the neighborhood. Anyway, Riley came inside screaming and crying because that girl had pushed Jenna into the mud and kicked her. Jenna's mom wasn't home, so I went up to the house to speak to the parents. They weren't receptive at all. So, now our little girls are going to learn how to whoop some bully ass."

His words infuriated me. "Let's go."

"What?" Savior asked.

"She's going to teach them since Batta's working tonight," Bronze explained.

Savior gave me a quick once over and nodded. "That's probably better. I was worried we'd have two Harley Quinns running around our neighborhood after Batta was finished with them."

Bronze led us downstairs to what I thought was going to be a private classroom but ended up being a large, open area with a boxing ring in the middle of the room. "It's what you think it is, or it was, so just leave it at that," Bronze said before I could ask.

"As long as it's not anymore, I'm good."

"All right, little princesses, let's get this party started. Where's my bad guy?"

Grant came out of the equipment room dressed in head-to-toe protective gear and climbed into the ring. "Take off your helmet so the girls can see it's really you," I whispered.

He did as I asked and waved to Riley and Jenna. "Hey there," he waved and smiled. Jenna returned his wave excitedly while Riley swooned.

"Oh, hell," I mumbled.

"Yeah, she's got a little crush on me."

"Shit. She might not be able to do this. She won't want to hurt you."

Grant threw his head back and laughed. "Have you met her?"

"Touché."

Turning my attention to the girls, I asked, "Do you know how to make a fist?"

Both girls nodded and curled their hands into a proper fist. "Very good." I wasn't surprised that they already knew some basics considering their ties to the MC.

"Now, I'm sure you both know where you can kick a man to hurt him. I like to call that the reset button. It works like a charm, every time. But, tonight, we're going to learn some ways to defend yourself against anyone, male or female. The first thing you want to do is get yourself into a good stance and keep your eyes on your attacker. A solid foundation will allow you to punch harder and keep you from toppling over. This is also when you want to yell 'No' or 'Get back.' Come on up here in the ring and let's give it a try."

I helped the girls position their feet and stabilize their center of gravity. "Now, we're going to put our hands out in front of us with our palms open like we're trying to stop someone from coming closer. This particular move will work well on someone who is close to the same height as you. It's called a down slap, and you want to do exactly what the name says—down slap." I turned to Grant, who'd replaced his helmet, and quickly slapped my hand over his face in a downward motion. "Just like that."

Both girls stared at me with wide eyes. "Grant's going to get down on his knees so you can try it. Jenna, let's have you go first, and then Riley can show us her down slap."

It took several tries before the girls really understood that they wouldn't hurt Grant. Once they were sure of his safety, they let the slaps fly.

"Good job!" I cheered. "Ready for the next move?"

"Yes!!" they squealed.

"Okay, who's seen the movie *Hotel Transylvania*?"

"Me!" they shouted in unison and raised their hands in the air.

"Good. You know how Dracula throws his cape up in front of his face? He does it super fast, and that's exactly what I want you to do—pretend like you're wearing a cape and throw your elbow up to cover your face. But, you're going to do it when you're close to your attacker so your elbow hits their nose. Now, here's the thing I want you both to understand. Grant is wearing protective gear that protects him and you. In a real situation, it might hurt a little to do this, but it will hurt the bad person much more and give you a chance to get away."

"Daddy and I say, 'Pain is temporary,' whenever I get hurt," Riley shared in a deep voice to sound like her dad causing me to laugh.

"That's a good one. I'll have to remember that," I said and clapped my hands. "Okay, ladies, show me how you throw a cape."

They took their turns throwing their capes at Grant. I clapped and cheered with each strike they made, genuinely proud of my little students.

"This next one is my personal favorite. It's called a throat punch, and again, that's exactly what it is. However, we aren't going to throw a direct punch at their throat."

"Like a jab?" Riley asked.

My eyebrows rose in surprise. "That's correct. We're not going to throw a jab at their throat, and here's why."

I threw a jab at Grant's throat, and he

immediately grabbed my arm and twisted it behind my back before my fist made contact with him. "Instead, we want to throw what's called a hammer fist. We're going to make a fist and use the side of it to strike the throat. You can do this from the side or directly in front of the attacker. This is the universal reset button on anyone. A direct hit to the throat requires minimal force to incapacitate someone. And because of that, we're going to practice this move on a dummy."

Savior moved one of the body opponent bags, aka BOB, into the corner of the ring. The girls each took a few turns striking their target. In reality, they wouldn't have hurt Grant, but I wanted to stress the effectiveness of the move.

"Last one, and then we're going to practice actual scenarios. This one is kind of gross, but it works. What you're going to do is slap both hands on the side of your attacker's face like this. See how my thumbs automatically went to the eye area? Here's the yucky part. You're going to press your thumbs into their eyes. Hard. This part is important to remember; the moment you feel their hands let go of you, shove them as hard as you can and run away."

"Eww! Momma said I wasn't supposed to touch my eyeball," Jenna said.

"She's right. But, you're not touching your eyeball; you're touching someone else's eyeball, and it's only because you need to get away," I explained.

"Are you sure?"

"I'm sure, but I'll talk to your mom about it when class is over," I offered.

"Okay. Thank you, Miss Tay."

Fucking hell. I hid my grimace and forced a smile. "How about you two call me Coach?"

"Okay, Coach," Riley said immediately.

"All right, let's get back to it. One of you can practice the eye gouge on Grant and the other can practice on BOB."

As I suspected, Riley sauntered right up to Grant and perfectly executed the maneuver. "You're going to have your hands full with her," I told Savior.

"I've heard that more times than I can count," he confessed.

"Good job, girls!! We're going to take a quick break so you can use the bathroom and get a drink of water. Then, we'll do some practice runs where Grant actually comes up and pretends to attack you."

I walked over and grabbed a bottle of water from my backpack while the girls ran off to the bathroom. When I stood and turned around, Trey was standing directly in front of me. His hands came around my waist and slid to my ass as he pulled me in for a quick kiss. Moving his lips to my neck, he asked against my skin, "What're you up to now?"

"Teaching some little girls how to kick some ass," I said proudly.

"Coach! We're ready!" Riley shouted.

"Go get 'em, Coach," Trey growled and slapped my ass.

"Hey! Not in front of the kids!" I scolded.

I climbed back into the ring with my eager students. "For this next part, Grant is going to try to attack you, and you're going to use what you learned in the first part of class to defend yourself and get away. Do you want me to go first?"

Jenna nodded, but Riley shook her head. "I wanna go first. Can I, Coach?"

"Of course you can," I said and gestured to the center of the ring.

It was all I could do to contain my laughter

when Grant dropped down and tried to run on his knees toward Riley. All humor vanished when Riley dropped to the floor and curled into a ball. Before anyone could get to her, Jenna flew across the ring, down slapped Grant, and followed up with a throat strike. Since Grant had been frozen in horror at Riley's reaction, he was completely caught off guard by Jenna and legitimately fell over on his side.

Savior swooped in and scooped Riley into his arms. "Are you okay, baby girl?"

Riley pushed away from his chest and turned her head to Jenna with a proud smile on her face. "Told ya it would work. He didn't even see you coming."

Grant sat up and pulled his helmet off. Chuckling, he glanced between both girls. "Y'all got me good."

Trey joined us in the ring. "What else did you girls learn tonight?"

Riley and Jenna excitedly showed him all the moves we went over. I was beyond impressed with how well they recalled each move and the important points associated with each one.

We practiced for another twenty minutes until Jenna's mother arrived to pick her up. I walked right up to her and introduced myself before explaining Jenna's concerns about touching eyeballs. She laughed and said she would make sure her daughter understood the difference. Then, she thanked me several times before finally taking her daughter home.

"You know who that is, don't you?" Trey asked.

"Yeah, Jenna and her mother, Kim."

He nodded with a little smirk on his face. "Kim is Kennedy's sister."

"And?" I asked.

"I'm just surprised you volunteered to teach her niece how to defend herself when you have such a clear dislike of Kennedy."

I scoffed, genuinely offended. "It's not the kid's fault that her aunt can't keep her boobs to herself. You can think what you want about me, but I would never hold the actions of one person against another person, especially a child."

I started to storm away from him, pissed off and a little hurt by his words. His big hand snagged my waist and pulled me back to him. "My bad, sugar tits. You're one of a kind; I should know that by now. Let's go back to your place and I'll make it up to you."

26

BATTA

The next morning, Tatum was downstairs in the kitchen when I woke up, already dressed in her ever-present tank top and tactical pants. "Morning," I rumbled and reached for the coffee pot.

She briefly glanced up from her computer to greet me before her attention was right back on the screen.

"You want to take a ride with me?"

"When?" she asked distractedly.

"Right now."

"Oh," she said and closed the lid to her laptop. "Uh, sure. Let me grab another shirt."

When she returned, I downed the rest of my coffee and headed out the door. She pulled her helmet on and climbed on the bike behind me. We rode for a little over an hour while I tried to decide if I was actually going to do it—take her to the one place I'd never taken anyone. "Fuck it," I mumbled to myself and pointed my bike in the right direction.

My gut tightened when I pulled onto the familiar street, and my forehead was covered in beads of sweat by the time I turned into the driveway.

"Where are we?" Tatum asked when we came to a stop.

I swallowed a few times and tried to clear the emotion from my throat. "My house."

"Your house? I thought you lived at the clubhouse."

"I do."

She cocked her head to the side and studied me. Stepping closer, she placed her hand on my chest. "This is your parents' house," she said knowingly.

I stared at the house that was once my home. No one had been inside since the day Hawk Black locked it up right after my dad was sentenced, but it didn't look that way from the outside. Hawk had arranged to have a service take care of the yard, and I'd continued doing the same when I turned eighteen and became the official owner of the property.

"The last time I was here was the last time I saw my mother alive," I told her.

"You never came back?" she asked.

I shook my head. "No, and I probably shouldn't have come today."

"Why did you?"

Tilting my head to the sky, I closed my eyes and took in a deep breath. "I don't know. I guess I wanted you to see it, so you could understand why I am the way I am when it comes to secrets and lies."

She remained silent while I glanced around the area and gathered my thoughts. Exhaling slowly, I pointed to the house that once belonged to Sarah and told her the story from the worst night of my life.

She wrapped her arms around me and listened intently to every word I spoke.

"Thank you for sharing this with me," she said softly. "Do you want to go inside?"

I shook my head and held up a key. "No, but I want you to. There's a bookshelf in the living room with three photo albums on it. Will you get those and bring them to me?"

"Of course. I'll be right back," she promised and took the key from my hand.

I turned away and stared at the road. I couldn't watch her open the door and enter my family's home. I couldn't risk the chance of catching a glimpse of the inside and seeing my old life frozen in time.

Tatum didn't waste any time. She was in and out of the house in a matter of minutes. "Here you go," she said and handed the three albums to me.

I ran my fingers over the front cover and stared reverently at the stack in my hand. The albums seemed much smaller than I remembered. "Thank you," I rasped. "I've wanted these for a long time, but I couldn't—"

"You're welcome," she interrupted, and followed up with a soft kiss.

I put the albums in my saddlebags and turned back to her. "You ready?"

"If you are."

I nodded slowly and let my eyes roam over the house one more time. "Yeah, I'm ready."

We rode for another half an hour before going

back to her place. I knew visiting the house would stir up emotions that were probably best left buried, but I had no idea how much just standing outside in the yard would wreck me.

I carried the albums upstairs to her bedroom and placed them on the dresser before dropping into the chair in the corner of the room and closing my eyes.

She climbed into my lap and ran her hand over my cheek. "I know today was hard for you. What can I do to make it better?"

"Give me your trust."

"Trey," she said hesitantly. "I can't tell you things about my job."

I shook my head and met her eyes. "I'm not talking about your job. I'm talking about you. We both know you could've gotten out of the restraints I used, but you chose not to. This will be different."

"Oh," she said as realization dawned. After a few long moments, she finally said, "I want to, but I don't know if I can."

"Why?" I would never hurt her, and I'd proven that many times since I met her. There had to be another reason behind her hesitation.

"I emasculate most men. I've come to terms

with that fact over the years and have no intentions of changing who I am to please others. But, there was a time in my life when I did doubt myself." She paused and took in a deep breath. Slowly exhaling, she continued, "A guy I dated tried to prove his manhood by 'putting me in my place.'"

I immediately tensed, furious that some prick would put his hands on her. She gently placed her hand on my chest to calm me. "Let me finish. I defended myself and immediately ended the relationship. I didn't really think anything of it other than I'd just picked a bad seed. But then it happened again. The second one had no problem telling me his reasoning when he tried to put his hands on me."

Tried. She said tried. I focused on that word as I tried to contain my anger. "Please tell me you kicked his ass."

She grinned. "Each one went to the hospital with a broken arm."

I leaned forward and kissed her forehead. "That's my girl," I said proudly. Leaning back, I met her eyes. "You're one hell of a woman, a badass in every way, but you don't emasculate me."

"I know."

"I have never put my hands on a woman in anger, and I never will," I said vehemently.

"I know."

"Good." I placed a chaste kiss on her lips and started to get up.

She pressed against my chest. "Wait."

"Yes?"

"I trust you," she said confidently.

I studied her, finding nothing but complete honesty in her eyes. "I'm going to do whatever I want to you. I'm going to call you filthy names and spank your ass. You'll be sore and covered in my come before I'm finished with you."

She shivered in my arms as her pupils dilated and her nipples turned to hard peaks beneath her thin tank top. "Okay," she whispered.

"Get naked and get on the bed. Don't move until I get back," I ordered.

When I returned from getting the paracord I kept on my bike, she was on the bed with her arms above her head and her legs splayed wide open with her knees bent.

"Very good, but I want you to sit up on your knees with your legs spread as wide as they'll go."

She did as I asked and silently waited for more instructions.

I pulled a chair in front of the bed and took a seat. Then, I pulled out her vibrator that I'd had since I had to collect her random list of shit and held it out to her. "I want to watch you fuck yourself like you would if no one was watching."

Her eyes filled with desire when she took the toy from my outstretched hand. "Do I have to stay in this position?"

"No, you can move however you want as long as I can see your cunt."

She nodded and dropped the vibrator onto the bed. First, she started massaging her tits before she concentrated on toying with her nipples.

"Can you suck your own nipples?"

"I've never tried," she breathed and lifted one tit to her mouth.

"Nice," I whispered. "Flick it with your tongue."

I almost came in my pants when she opened her mouth and lapped at her nipple with fervor.

"How does that feel?"

"It feels good. It's making my pussy so wet. I want to touch it, to shove something in it."

"Do it. Fuck that pussy for me, you needy little slut."

She grabbed the toy, turned it on, and shoved it into her cunt, releasing a loud groan. Without my guidance, she started to fuck it, moving up and down like she was riding my cock.

"Trey, oh, oh, please. Please hold it for me."

I knew I couldn't get that close to her and keep myself in check. "No. You have two minutes to make yourself come, or you won't be coming tonight."

"Fuck," she cursed and fell onto her back. She used one hand to thrust the toy in and out of her channel while the other furiously rubbed her clit. Within thirty seconds, she exploded, coming with my name on her lips.

The moment she was finished, I yanked the vibrator from her hands and tossed it across the room. Hoisting her to the top of the bed, I made quick work of securing her wrists to the headboard, much tighter than the previous times. I pulled my cock out and spit in my hand before I fisted it and pumped several times. With one knee on either side of her chest, I pushed her tits together and thrust my cock between the two luscious mounds. "I've been dying to fuck these tits," I groaned.

She watched my every move but didn't utter a word. Her mouth was hanging open and her eyes were glazed over, likely still recovering from her orgasm.

I didn't try to fight it when I felt the tingle in my balls. Instead, I picked up the pace and took my cock in my hand to finish myself off so I could spray my come where I wanted it to go—all over her perky tits. After squeezing out the last dregs, I looked down at my work and proudly rubbed my seed into her skin. "Fuck you look good covered in me."

She smiled and relaxed back into the bed. "Oh, no, sugar tits, we're just getting started."

With that, I moved back and grabbed the paracord. After securing both ankles to the headboard, I shoved two pillows under her ass, leaving her completely open and exposed for my ministrations.

"This seems to be a favorite position for you," she smarted.

"Do I need to gag you?" I asked with an arched brow then shook my head. "No, I want to hear you beg for mercy."

She gasped in surprise, but I didn't acknowledge it as I got off the bed and retrieved the bottle of olive oil I brought up when I got the paracord.

Climbing back onto the bed, I looked down at the sight before me. Perfect tits, glistening cunt, and what I assumed was a virgin asshole. Dropping some oil onto my finger, I pressed it against her ass. "Anybody had you here?"

She shook her head repeatedly. "No. You're going to be the first."

I couldn't stop myself from pressing my finger inside as I groaned. "Fuck yes, I am."

With that, I leaned down and sucked her clit into my mouth while I pumped my finger in and out of her tight hole. "Relax and let my finger fuck your ass."

Eventually, she did relax, and I added a second finger, scissoring the two to stretch her for me. All the while, I lapped and sucked at her clit, even biting it a time or two.

I felt the walls of her pussy tighten and knew she was close to coming again. Before she could, I slipped a third finger into her ass. "Oh, fuck, Trey. It's too much."

I continued to pump them in and out and

lavish her clit. "Is it really? Or does your greedy cunt love it?"

She was panting and fighting against the restraints. "Trey. I-I, oh, fuck."

The moment her cunt started to spasm, I pulled my fingers from her ass and filled it with my cock. She started to scream, but it died on her lips when my fingers landed on her clit and started rubbing circles.

"I'm gonna—"

"You're going to scream my name while your cunt comes from having your ass fucked by my big cock."

"Yes! Yes! Trey!"

Seconds later, her orgasm hit, and her muscles started squeezing me, almost to the point of pain. Just when I thought I wouldn't be able to take anymore, she relaxed. The built-up pressure relieved as my come shot out of me and my body was overcome with pleasure.

Dropping my weight onto her, I kissed my way from her neck to her mouth. Once I was finished devouring her lips, I pressed my forehead to hers and looked deep into her warm, amber eyes. "Thank you," I whispered.

27

BATTA

Two weeks passed and with Josie not around as a reminder, I'd almost forgotten that Tatum was in Devil Springs on some kind of work assignment. During the week, she worked regular nine-to-five hours at the bookstore. Then, she spent the evenings and weekends with me. She even came and worked out at the gym a few nights when I volunteered to close for Savior because his baby girl was sick.

However, I had an errand to run on Saturday, and she couldn't come with me. Turns out, I didn't need to worry about what to tell her. When I came downstairs, Tatum had her face buried in her laptop and didn't seem like she would be coming up for air any time soon. After having a cup of coffee and a bite to eat, I told her, "I'll be back in a few hours," and gave her a quick kiss on the lips.

"Okay," she mumbled and went right back to the screen, barely acknowledging me.

I hated this particular ride, but I would have hated myself more for not taking it. I pulled into the lot and took a deep breath. I'd made the same trip hundreds of times, and it never got any easier.

It was the same routine every single time. Very little had changed over the years. After going through multiple checks and locked doors, then waiting an additional thirty minutes, I was finally sitting in front of my father.

"Hey, Dad," I greeted and reached out to shake his hand. That was the only contact they would allow. The last time my dad hugged me was at the clubhouse right before he turned himself in. It didn't matter how old I was or how many years had passed; it was one of the things I missed the most.

"Trey," he rumbled with a slight smile. "How're you doing, Son?"

"I'm good," I said quietly and reached into

my pocket. Pulling out the small photo, I placed it on the table and pushed it to my dad.

Inhaling sharply, he carefully picked it up and traced his finger over my mother's face. "You went to the house."

"I couldn't go inside," I confessed. "I had someone go in and get the photo albums for me. Should've done it a long time ago, but—"

"You don't have to explain yourself to me." He studied the picture for a few moments longer before placing it on the table and pushing it back to me.

"That's yours. I had copies made and kept the original at home."

"Thank you," he said and continued to stare at the picture.

"Dad," I said uncomfortably. "I need to ask you something."

"What's troubling you, Son?"

"Uh, I had a dream a few weeks ago. About Mom. I've had dreams about her before, but this one was different. It was like I was talking to her. And she told something. Um, and I want to know if it's true."

"What did she say?" he asked, and I got the

feeling that he already knew what I was going to say.

"She said that Sarah told y'all about her ex-husband. That the club was trying to help her."

Dad sat back in his chair and visibly swallowed. "Yes, we knew about him. And, yes, the club was trying to help her. We were trying to do things the right way, and it completely backfired."

"Why didn't you tell me?"

"Trey, at the time, you were sixteen years old. We didn't want you worried or scared. I hate to say it, but we thought, even if he did come after Sarah, the chances of you or your mother being in danger were slim to none. I should've demanded that your mother stay away from that house or insisted on having a prospect at the house when I wasn't there. It's the biggest regret of my life."

"Dad," I said and reached out for his hand. "That's not why I asked. I want to know if…I wanted to know if it was really Mom," I whispered.

He patted my hand. "It was. She talks to me when she has something to say that I need to hear."

"I miss her."

"I do, too," he said and sighed. "But, remember, she's with you every day."

"That's what she said."

"Your mother was a magnificent woman. It doesn't surprise me at all that she's found a way to still be a part of our lives. And speaking of magnificent women, I heard you got yourself a girl."

I snorted and shook my head. "I should've known Leigh would tell you." Leigh had gotten licensed as a minister not long after my dad was sentenced so she could visit him without it counting against his allotted visitations.

I cleared my throat and shifted uncomfortably. "Yeah, I've met someone."

"Tell me about her."

I chuckled. "She's hard to put into words. She's, uh, she's pretty badass, to be honest. Beautiful, strong, a bit of a smart-ass. You'd like her."

"Wish I could meet her, Son. If she's still around in a few years, maybe I can," he said solemnly.

"Yeah, I don't know how long she'll be around. She's only here because of her job."

"Leigh said Jonah's girl was only in town because of her job but look how that turned out."

"River's a nurse. They need nurses everywhere. Tatum's job isn't like that."

"Do you want her to stay?" he asked.

I didn't have to think about it. "Yes."

"Are you willing to go with her if she can't stay?"

"I don't know," I said honestly. "As much as I don't want her to go, I can't leave the club either. They're my family."

"Be sure you tell her what you just told me. Don't wait until it's too late or assume she knows."

"Mom knew how much you loved her," I said quietly.

"I know she did. And I knew how much she loved me. She never asked me to find a job that would keep me at home, and I've spent every day since her death wishing she had. Maybe she would still be here."

"Or maybe I would be without both parents. You can't play the 'what if' game, Dad. You're the one who taught me that."

He snorted. "Yeah, but it's not always easy to take your own advice." Then, he clapped his hands together. "So, tell me about the rest of the club. How's everyone doing? Any more trouble with the gym?"

Before I was ready, our time was up. Saying goodbye to him never got easier, either. I don't know how he handled it, but I rode hell-bent for leather all the way to Devil Springs and usually spent the rest of the day beating the hell out of something with my fists or my bat.

Instead of going to the gym or the clubhouse, I headed to Tatum's place. I knew she would be willing to help me work out my frustrations without questioning me about them. It was one of the things I loved about her.

Loved. Yes, I loved her. And after hearing what my dad had to say, I was going to tell her sooner rather than later.

Upon this realization, I let off the gas and slowed to a much safer speed, even though I couldn't wait to get to her.

When I arrived at her place, I was surprised she wasn't waiting at the back door for me. Since she could hear me coming, she always met me at the door. I knocked several times, but she didn't answer. I knew better than to walk into the house and risk startling her, so I pulled out my phone and called her. It rang several times before going to her voicemail.

Next, I called Coal. "Hey, brother, can you look out front and tell me if Tatum's truck is parked in the lot?"

"Yeah, man, just a sec." I heard him moving around and a few moments later, he said, "It's not here."

"Will you double check and see if she's at the store?"

"Sure. Everything okay?"

"I just got back to her place, and her truck's not here. As far as I know, she didn't plan on going anywhere, but she's not answering her phone."

"She's not answering the door here, and there aren't any lights on."

"Thanks, brother. Let me know if you happen to see her," I said and ended the call as an uneasy feeling settled in my gut.

"Fuck it," I muttered and reached for the door, giving the knob a cursory turn. Unexpectedly, I found it to be unlocked. And that's when I knew something was wrong.

I pulled my gun from its holster and chambered a round right before I dialed Copper.

"I need you and anyone available to get over to Tatum's place right now."

"Be right there, brother," he vowed.

Slowly, I made my way into the house, quietly and methodically moving from room to room. Once I cleared the main level, I started to go up the stairs, but the door to the basement caught my eye.

Throwing caution to the wind, I hauled ass down the stairs as fast as I could and went straight for the wine cellar. Crashing through there like a bull in a china shop, I reached for the shelves attached to the rear wall and pulled as hard as I could. When nothing happened, I started pulling the bottles from the shelves and carelessly tossing them to the floor.

Suddenly, I heard several clicks, as if multiple locks were being unlocked at the same time. I pushed against the wall again, and that time it turned with ease. I stepped inside and quickly closed the secret door behind me.

I wanted to yell for her, but I didn't want to give away my location in case I could be heard from outside the secret space, which appeared to be a tunnel. Or so I thought. Lights illuminated the passage with each step I took until I found myself staring at another door.

I yanked it open and stepped into a pitch-black room. "Tatum," I whispered. "It's Trey. Baby, are you in here?"

A light clicked on, and a woman who looked just like Tatum stepped out of the shadows. With my gun aimed at her head, I demanded, "Who the fuck are you, and where is Tatum?"

The woman started shaking and crying. "Nooo! They got her! I know they got her!" As if I wasn't pointing a gun at her, she charged me and started shaking me by my shirt. "You have to help her!"

"Woman! I won't ask again. Who are you? Who has Tatum?"

"I'm her sister!" she screamed and beat her fists against my chest. "Call Luke! Now!"

"Batta!" Copper's deep voice echoed down the hall. "I've got Luke on the line. The house is clear. Come back to the wine cellar and bring Josie with you."

I continued to stare at the crying woman in complete and total shock. I'd met Tatum's sister, and she was not the woman I met, but she looked almost identical to Tatum. She wasn't as tall and her muscles weren't as defined, but there were far more similarities than there were differences.

"Batta!" Copper roared. "Now!"

I gestured toward the door with my gun. "Go."

She didn't hesitate and almost ran for the secret door. She reached to the side and pressed a button, causing the door to swivel open with ease. "Luke! Let me talk to Luke," she cried.

Copper shoved the phone into her trembling hands as I stepped back into the light. "The fuck is going on?"

Copper shook his head. "I don't know all the details yet, but that," he nodded to the woman, "is Tatum's sister Josie. Luke won't give the identity of the other woman."

"'Adrianna.' Cristofano called her 'Adrianna'," I mumbled.

"Here," Josie said and held out the phone. "He wants to talk to you."

Copper put the phone to his ear and took a few steps away. Josie pointed her red-rimmed eyes, ones so much like her sister's, at me. "My sister loves you."

"I love your sister," I said softly.

"We have to get her back," she cried.

"We will."

"Church. Right here, right now," Copper ordered. "Josie, Luke wants you to go back into your hideout. I'm going to have two armed men guarding you while we go get your sister."

"O-okay," she said shakily.

"This is my brother, Bronze, and my cousin, Coal. Coal is also Luke's nephew. They'll be sitting right out here in the wine cellar, but I need you to go on in there now," Copper said gently.

"Okay, just, please hurry," she pled.

"We will. I promise you that," he vowed.

Once she was gone, Copper laid it all out for us. "Tatum's real sister, Josie, married Sheldon Morgan who was involved in selling human organs on the black market. According to Luke, Josie knew nothing about it until she discovered a woman locked in what she thought was a storage room in their basement. That woman was Adrianna Smith, also known as Clarise Barrington. Sheldon came home in the middle of Josie's discovery. Adrianna ran up the stairs and kicked Sheldon in the back just as he fired a shot at Josie. The shot missed her, but his body collided with Josie before he fell to the floor and dropped the gun. Josie got the gun and put a bullet in

Sheldon before she lost consciousness beside him. Tatum got there only seconds after the shots were fired."

"How the hell did they end up in Devil Springs? And where is Adrianna now?" Judge asked.

"They knew Sheldon wasn't acting on his own, but they had no leads. Someone out there wanted Adrianna's organs and was willing to pay a lot of money for them. In order to protect Adrianna while trying to catch the other partners, they gave bogus information to the media, filed contradictory police reports, and had Adrianna and Josie swap identities. Luke sent them here in case he needed to call on us to help protect them —which he ultimately did," Copper explained.

"I don't really give a fuck about the why of it right now!" I bellowed. "We need to find my woman! Right the fuck now! We don't know how long she's been gone, or who has her!"

Copper exhaled slowly and glanced at Judge and Bronze before focusing on me. "They do know how long she's been gone. And they do know who has her."

"What?" I bellowed and swiped an entire row of wine bottles from the shelf beside me.

"Tatum and Adrianna used themselves as bait. Lu—" Copper's words were cut off by the feral roar of outrage I released.

Glass shattered, wood splintered, and blood spilled before I was taken to the ground by two big bodies.

"Trey," Copper gritted out as he and Judge struggled to contain me. "We got you. We've always got you."

Those words. Those were the same words they said to me on the night I lost my mom. They didn't let me down then, and I knew they wouldn't this time.

28

LUKE

If I had a stroke because of Tatum Cross, I was going to make sure she was the one tasked with wiping my ass for the rest of my life. The woman was damn good at her job and more loyal than anyone I knew, but she was the most impatient pain in the ass to ever exist. It was much worse with this case because it hit her on a personal level. And not just because it involved her sister. No, Tatum was rushing this case because she'd fallen in love with a biker, and keeping secrets from him was eating her up inside, even if she wasn't ready to admit it to anyone, including herself.

Against my better judgment, I helped her get all of her ducks in a row so she could toss herself out there as a piece of bait for organ traders. Hell, we were both probably going to get fired for this stunt, even if we were successful. And there was a good chance we wouldn't be, but I also knew there was no way I could stop her. She was going through with her plans with or without my help, and I couldn't in good conscience let her go it alone. That's not how our team worked.

Part of me thought Tatum's plan was borderline genius, while the other part of me thought it was utterly insane. If it didn't work, we would tank the entire investigation, but more importantly, innocent lives could be lost. I couldn't let that happen. So, I called in every possible favor I could and made a few deals with the devil to put her plan in motion.

It wasn't anywhere near as solid as our normal plans. Nothing was foolproof, and our backup plan had the same chances as a snowflake in hell, but it was the best we could do, and we were going with it.

In exchange for the destruction of some records, Luca's uncle, Giovanni Peccati, agreed to front the money and put the word out that his daughter was in desperate need of a kidney transplant. Fictitious medical records were created, fake social media pages popped up, and word was spread on the dark web. And, most importantly, we secured our own surgeon, which was crucial to the deal going through.

Within days, one of Nolan's associates, Chandler, contacted Giovanni and scheduled a meeting. Giovanni met with Chandler and handed over the file we prepared for him, along with a deposit of fifty thousand dollars in cash.

Once the deal was made, we knew Nolan and Simon would move quickly. Giovanni was offering too much money for them to refuse. With the money and most of the legwork out of the way, Tatum knew they wouldn't pass up the chance to use Adrianna as the donor for a member of the very family she betrayed them for. I had to agree with her; it was poetic justice at its finest.

So, with a plan held together with bubblegum and dry-rotted rope, we dropped the bait in the water and prayed for a bite. It was going to take the good Lord above, all nine lives, and a stroke of the strongest luck to pull it off, but we were nothing if not determined.

I called Phoenix and told him that Tatum was on her way to pick up her sister because we needed to move her to a safe house closer to our home base so we could easily question her if needed. Tatum arrived at the Croftridge clubhouse on schedule and left with Adrianna as planned.

Once the girls made it to Cedar Valley, they stopped for lunch at a hole-in-the-wall diner near the airport. As planned, Monica, a woman on our payroll, tipped off Nolan's man, Chandler.

The girls got back on the road. Dave and Jack were following them at a safe distance, and Matt was tracking them via satellite. It wasn't long before they picked up a tail, as expected.

This was the part of the plan I had the biggest problem with. Once the girls were cornered, there was no guarantee they would take Tatum with them. It was highly likely they would save themselves the trouble and kill her on the spot. And, I didn't care if it meant blowing the case wide fucking open, there was no way I was letting that happen on my watch.

Before any of us were ready, everything kicked into high gear. One second everything was fine, and the next, I heard the sound of a large impact followed by the live feed from Tatum's dashcam turning end over end.

"Fuck! Fuck! Fuck! They've been hit!" I

screamed into my headpiece. "Get in there now! Now!"

I heard Jack's vehicle accelerate, but it did nothing to calm me. "Fucking hurry, man!" I yelled and put my fist through the dry wall.

Tires screeched to a halt followed by Dave's booming voice. "Go, Jack! Go after them!"

His labored breathing filled my ears before deafening silence took over. "Dave? Talk to me, Dave."

"No," he whispered. "No, no, no."

"What? Tell me what I can't see, Dave."

"I think Adrianna's dead! And they took Tatum!"

"Fuck!" I roared. "Matt! I need a location! Gus, get us a bird in the air! Somebody get local PD on the phone. We need an ambo on scene, now!"

29

TATUM

Tears streaked down my face. I didn't know if Adrianna was still alive. If she was, I knew she was seriously injured, and I prayed Dave and Jack got to her in time. I swore I would keep her safe, and I was going to annihilate anyone and everyone who played a part in making me break my promise.

After my truck was rammed and sent rolling off the road, I was unceremoniously yanked through the window and tossed into the back of a cargo van. Goon One quickly cuffed my hands behind my back while Goon Two sped off down the road.

I let the anger and rage fuel me with a determination that burned hotter than a thousand suns. Every last one of these motherfuckers was going down.

Quietly rolling to my side, I brought my knees to my chest. Then, I rolled to my back and maneuvered my cuffed hands over my feet. With my cuffed hands in front of me, I reached up and plucked a bobby pin from my hair. In less than a minute, I was free.

Immediately, I reached into my front pocket and pulled out the tiny device that was the key to our success. I pressed the button that would send my GPS location to Luke and the other members of my team and slipped it into my back pocket. Then, I coughed loudly to cover the noise as I loosely cuffed my hands behind my back. One good shake and the cuffs would slide right off, but Dumb and Dumber didn't need to know that.

For added effect, I coughed a few more times. "Hey, dipshits! Can I get some water?"

When neither responded, I continued. "Hellloooo! Fuckfaces! Are you deaf or just stupid?"

"Hmm, what's the catchiest song I can sing at the top of my lungs?" I wondered aloud. And then I proceeded to sing *Baby Shark*. I only made it to the third verse before Goon Two thrust a bottle of water in my face.

"Oh, how thoughtful of you, sir," I taunted and slowly took a few sips of water. "Thank you."

He smirked. "You're not welcome." Then, pain exploded across my face when he slammed his fist into my cheek. "Keep your fucking mouth shut, bitch."

I smiled, with my mouth closed, and nodded as I played out fifteen different ways to kill him in my mind.

After he returned to the front of the van, I cataloged my assessment of him. He wasn't much taller than me, but he did outweigh me by at least forty pounds of fat. His eyes were cold, but not calculating, which led me to believe he was nothing more than hired help and likely disposable. As far as I could tell, he only had one gun tucked into the back of his pants. I could kill him with the pins holding my bun in place before he ever got his hands on his weapon.

Twisting around, I leaned as far as I could to the side without being noticed so I could get a look at Goon One. He was pretty much what I expected—a replica of Goon Two. Maybe they were twins. I opened my mouth to ask but thought better of it when pain shot through my cheek.

Every so often, I tapped the GPS locator in my pocket to let the team know where I was, and that I was still okay. I probably tapped it far more often than I should have, but I didn't have anything else to do, and sending a signal to them took my mind off of Adrianna for a few moments.

I wasn't worried about Josie. After showing him the wine cellar and making sure he noticed the faint seam along the wall, I knew Trey would find her and make sure she was safe. And that's when I realized I loved him. Because he would put his life on the line to save someone just because they meant something to me. I also knew he wouldn't sit idly by while I was in danger. I just hoped all would be said and done by the time he caught up with us.

I HAD NO IDEA HOW LONG WE'D BEEN DRIVING, BUT I was certain several hours had passed when the van finally came to a stop. I hit the button in my back pocket three times in quick succession to let

Luke know we were at a stopping point, and then I prepared myself for the unknown.

"Hey, shitheads, any chance I can pee while we're stopped?" I called out.

"No," one of them grunted.

"Fine, but don't be mad when I piss in your van."

"You should've fucking knocked her out."

"If she doesn't shut her fucking mouth, I will."

I held in my snort and kept my mouth shut. Finally, after long minutes, Goon One said, "There he is. Let's do this."

I hit the button in my pocket five times to let Luke and the team know I was about to be handed off to another party. With any luck, the team would swarm in the moment they pulled me from the van.

When the rear doors swung open, Goon Two yanked me out and dropped me onto my feet. "Here she is, sir."

"She's not who you were sent to get, but she'll do," a familiar voice said.

I turned and gasped. "Sheldon."

"What's the matter, Tatum? You look as though you've seen a ghost."

"Well, seeing as how you're supposed to be dead, I'd say that's a fitting observation."

"Clearly, I'm not. Come along; we don't have time for idle chit-chat," he said and reached for my arm.

That's when I noticed our location. We were at what appeared to be a private landing strip. A Learjet sat no more than fifty yards away waiting for us to board.

Oh, hell no. If I got on that plane, they'd never find me. I glanced around again, but there was nowhere for me to run, nowhere to take cover. Fuck, I needed to somehow stall them.

Tensing my abdomen, I grimaced and let out a loud fart, followed by a groan. "I knew I shouldn't have eaten that gas station burrito." Hoping for the best, I tensed again and let out another fart. "Does that fancy plane have a bathroom on it?" I asked and started to hop around. "Come on, man. Stuff wants out. Now!"

"Fuck that! I'm not smelling your rotten ass for the next few hours," Sheldon declared.

"Dude, I can feel it coming!" I shouted urgently. "I gotta go!"

Goon One produced a bucket from the back of the cargo van. "She can use this, boss."

Sheldon's lips curled in disgust. "Fine. Take her over on the other side of the van. I don't want to see, or hear, any of it."

Goon One made a disgusted noise in the back of his throat but led me to the far side of the van.

"You're going to have to help me with my pants," I groaned and managed to push out another fart right as he bent forward.

He covered his mouth and nose with his hand. "Theo! Get over here and help me."

Theo, also known as Goon Two, came to assist his friend. "Help me get her pants down before she shits all over herself, and he makes us clean it up."

When Theo reached for the waistband of my pants, I took my chance. I shook the cuffs off and kneed him in the balls while simultaneously pulling out one of my hair pins. While Theo hit the ground, I shoved the hair pin through Goon One's neck. Quickly pivoting, I kicked Theo right under his chin, effectively knocking him out.

He hit the ground with a thud, and I pulled his gun from the back of his pants. That's when Goon One reached for his own weapon. I slammed the butt of the gun into the side of his head as hard as I could and took his pistol once he was down. Then, I sat on the bucket and waited for Sheldon or my team to appear.

I was betting the team would show first, but part of me hoped it would be Sheldon so I could shoot him once or twice. I'd never liked him anyway. To be on the safe side, I continued to groan and make farting noises while I sat on the bucket kicking my feet.

And then it happened. Shiny, pretentious loafers appeared in my periphery. "What in the —?" Sheldon started, but his words were interrupted by the bullet I put in his chest.

"Who's on the plane?" I demanded.

He shook his head and reached for something in his suit jacket. "I always hated you."

I took great pleasure in blowing a hole in his hand. "Who. Is. On. The. Plane?"

"N-n-no one," he stammered. "Just the p-p-pilot."

Before I could discern whether or not he was telling the truth, the sound of several engines approaching filled my ears, followed by the beautiful sound of helicopter blades chopping through the air.

Three black SUVs came to a screeching halt, just as two helicopters landed on the far side of the plane. Jack jumped out of the first SUV and ran full tilt toward me. "I'm fine! Clear the plane!" I yelled, keeping my gun trained on Sheldon.

"Tatum," Luke called from my side. "You're okay," he breathed and pulled me in for a hug.

"Of course I am. You weren't worried, were you?"

"You know I was," he confessed and ruffled my hair.

"Adrianna?" I asked quietly, hesitantly.

"She's in the hospital. Was hurt pretty bad in the wreck, but she should make it."

I closed my eyes and exhaled in relief. "Josie?"

"You know she's fine."

"Yeah, but I needed to hear it."

"Plane's clear. Only one on board is the pilot," Dave called.

"Sweet. Let's go," I said and started for the plane.

"Whoa! Where do you think you're going?" Luke asked.

"Uh, to the private island to get Simon and Nolan."

Luke shook his head. "Absolutely not."

"Are you fuc—?"

"A team is going. But you're not on that team," he said firmly.

"You know, after the day I've had, I'm kind of okay with that," I confessed.

"Good, because you need to be seen by a doctor. You've been in a car wreck, and I'm going to take a wild guess and say your cheek is probably broken."

At the mention of my cheek, the throbbing returned full force and I grimaced. "Yeah," I conceded. "You're probably right."

"Where exactly are—?" Once again, I was interrupted, but this time it was by the sound of another helicopter.

Shielding my eyes with my hand, I looked toward the sky. "That's not one of ours," I said to Luke.

"No, it's not," he agreed, but he didn't seem concerned.

"Do you know who it is?" I pressed.

"I do," he smirked.

"Damn it, Luke."

"Payback's a bitch. Remember that the next time you decide to be a pain in my ass," he said and started to whistle as he casually strolled away.

In the next instant, I was hit with a solid force

and surrounded by strong arms I was very familiar with. "Trey," I breathed and sagged against him.

"I'm so pissed at you," he growled. "But right now, I'm just glad you're okay because I fucking love you," he said and gently tilted my face toward his. The relief in his eyes quickly morphed into red, hot rage. "Who hurt you?"

It was wrong. I knew it before I did it, but at that moment, I didn't care. My man was upset and needed an outlet. Plus, he could get away with it. "He did," I said and pointed to Goon Two cuffed on the ground.

"I don't have my bat, so I'll have to do this the old-fashioned way," Trey said but didn't seem disappointed in the least. Theo's eyes widened comically as Trey stalked over to him. Faster than I thought possible, Trey flipped Theo onto his stomach and used his bare hands to break both bones in his right forearm. Then, he bent low and whispered something in his ear. Before he was finished, a large wet spot began to form on the front of Theo's pants.

"Damn it, Tatum!" Luke shouted. "Was that really necessary?"

I shrugged. "Meh, depends on who you ask."

Luke pinched the bridge of his nose and shook his head. Then, he focused on Trey. "Will you take her to the hospital Adrianna is at? Make sure she is seen by a medical professional first. And don't let her out of your sight."

Trey smirked. "That I can do. Come on, sugar tits, you can start explaining on the way."

With his arm around my shoulders, he led me to the waiting helicopter. "Um, where did this come from?"

"My brother, Shaker, owns it," he yelled as he helped me inside.

When my eyes landed on the pilot, my forehead scrunched in confusion. "I haven't seen him around the clubhouse."

Trey chuckled and handed me a headset. Once we both had ours in place, he said, "He's from the Croftridge chapter."

"I see. And how did you boys manage to get clearance to land in the middle of an FBI operation?"

Trey winked. "That's classified."

When we arrived at the hospital, I begged

and pleaded for him to take me to Adrianna, but he insisted we go to the ER first. "If you go up there before getting medical attention, it will do nothing but upset Adrianna. Is that what you want?"

"No," I huffed. It most certainly was not what I wanted.

"They know you're coming, and they have a room waiting for you. It won't take long."

He was right. My ass didn't even get a chance to land in a chair in the waiting room before we were taken back to an exam room. And then, Nurse Let Me Press My Tits On Your Arm walked into the room.

"You've got to be kidding me," I mumbled.

"Hi, I'm Kennedy," she chirped.

"Hello, Kennedy. I'm tired, cranky, and in a lot of pain. So, if you could keep your tits off my man's arm and get this show on the road, I'll do my best to be somewhat pleasant."

Her eyes widened and her cheeks flushed. "Excuse me?"

"I didn't stutter. Take it for what it was and move on. You gonna x-ray this shit?" I asked and circled the air in front of my swollen cheek.

She cleared her throat. "Let me check with the doctor. Do you have any other injuries?"

I shrugged. "I was in a rollover accident moments before I was handcuffed and thrown into the back of a van where I was punched in the face by a man much bigger than me. In other words, I don't fucking know."

"Tatum," Trey scolded.

"What? I don't fucking know. I didn't have time to do a full body assessment while I was trying to keep myself alive."

"I'll just grab one of the doctors. Just a moment," Kennedy said and left the room.

"You really don't like her, do you?" Trey asked.

"Eh, I'm not sure if I don't like her or if I just like fucking with her. She's scared of me. She should've never let me know that."

He laughed and stepped between my legs. Gently running his hands up my back, he urged me to lean against his chest. "Really, baby, are you hurt anywhere else?"

"I don't think so. I'm sore, and I'm sure it will be worse tomorrow, but nothing stands out other than my cheek," I admitted.

Thirty minutes later, I was diagnosed with a fractured cheekbone and sent on my way with a prescription for pain medication I wouldn't take and a note excusing me from work for a few days. I couldn't wait to see Luke's face when I turned that in.

By the time we made it to Adrianna's room, I was ready for a hot bath and a long nap. The adrenaline was long gone, and I was fading fast. To my surprise, Copper and Judge were sitting in chairs outside of her door.

"What're you doing?" I asked.

"Making sure no one bothers your 'sister'," Copper replied slowly.

"And my other sister?" I asked.

Copper grinned. "She's in there, too, anxiously awaiting your arrival."

With that, they got to their feet and Copper opened the door for me. "Tatum!" Josie screamed and made a beeline for me.

Trey stepped in front of me and intercepted her. "Easy. She's sore."

Then, he moved out of the way, and Josie wrapped me in a gentle hug. "Are you okay?" she cried.

"Yeah, I'm good. How's Adrianna?" I asked and studied the still figure in the bed.

"She has a few broken bones, a concussion, and they're keeping a close eye on her spleen. If it continues to swell, they may have to remove it."

"Has she been awake at all?" I asked.

"Oh, yes, she's been awake almost the whole time. The nurse just gave her some pain medication, and she dozed off a few minutes later."

"Sit down, baby," Trey insisted and pushed a chair against the backs of my legs.

"Can you tell me what happened?" Josie whispered.

I nodded. "Yeah, I can tell you most of it. Uh, you're not going to like this part, but, um, Sheldon is still alive. Or he was. I shot him a couple of times, so he might have died; but, when I left he was still very much alive."

"What?!" she shrieked.

"Yep," I nodded. "I didn't see that one coming either."

"What the hell was he doing there?"

"That part will have to wait, but you'll have all the answers by morning."

"Oh, okay," she said and glanced around the small room. "Are you going to go and come back?"

I snorted. "Seriously, Josie? I don't care if I have to sleep on the floor; I'm not going anywhere tonight."

THE SOUND OF THE DOOR OPENING WOKE ME FROM a deep sleep. Thankfully, Trey had been able to acquire two cots for the room—Josie was on one while he and I were doing our best to fit on the other one. Copper and Judge had been replaced by Bronze and Coal, but just knowing two men were out there standing guard was what allowed me to sleep so soundly.

I opened my eyes to see Luke quietly entering the room with two cups of coffee in his hands. "One of those better be for me," I said, my voice raspy from sleep.

"It is," he whispered.

"What time is it?" I asked as I extricated myself from Trey and sat up.

"A little before six," he said with a grin.

"Just in time for the six o'clock news. How convenient," I said knowingly and turned on the television.

"Something tells me they have a good story this morning."

"Yes!" I whisper-shouted and pumped my fist in the air. "Now, give me the coffee and let me watch in peace."

"We're coming to you this morning with breaking news. Media mogul Simon Barrington and British billionaire Nolan Morgan have been taken into custody for their involvement in acquiring and selling human organs on the black market. Morgan's son, Sheldon, was also arrested yesterday in connection with the case. Details are still coming in, but trusted sources tell us Barrington's private island and Morgan's superyachts were instrumental in illegally procuring and transplanting human organs. We'll continue to keep you updated as more information comes in."

A soft gasp had me turning to look at Adrianna. Tears were pouring from her eyes. "My father did this? Why?"

"I think you know why," I said carefully.

"Because I ran away?" she asked and then gasped as if something suddenly registered to her. "It was Sheldon! He never told me who he was marrying me off to. They did this to get back at me."

"We can't say that for sure without talking to

him, but it looks that way," I said softly and made my way over to her.

"It wasn't Cristofano's fault," she whispered and started to cry. "The whole time I blamed him." She sucked in a deep breath and immediately grimaced in pain. "I'm sorry I didn't tell you about my family."

"It's okay. I know why you didn't."

"Will he get in trouble?" she asked quietly.

"Trouble for what?" I asked. "It's not uncommon for the child of someone rich and famous to change their name or use an alias for privacy reasons. There's nothing wrong with that."

"But we didn't do it the right way," she whispered.

"I'll take care of that," I promised.

"Thank you," she managed to say before she choked on a sob and groaned in pain.

Reaching out, I pressed the button for the nurse. Then, I carefully took her hand in mine and gave it a gentle squeeze. "I'm so sorry you got hurt."

She shook her head. "Don't you dare apologize to me," she said vehemently. "I knew what the risks were when I agreed to help. And it was worth it. You got 'em."

"*We* did," I corrected. "We sure as fuck did."

"Unfortunately, it's not over yet," Luke interjected, causing Adrianna's face to fall.

"The hard part is over, but we need to keep you in protective custody until we're sure you're safe, meaning after the trial," I explained.

"How long will that be?" she asked.

I shrugged. "There's no way for us to know that."

"Will we have to go somewhere else?" she asked, and her chin started to quiver.

"Um," I started and turned back to Luke. Lowering my voice, I pointed out, "The safe house was never compromised."

"For now, when you're released from the hospital, we'll have Tatum stay with you and Josie at the safe house. We have time to work out the rest," he offered.

30

BATTA

Adrianna was released from the hospital a few hours after the story hit the news. Tatum and Josie both expressed their concerns about her leaving the hospital too soon.

"I'm sure River or Kennedy would be happy to stop by and check on Adrianna," I said without thinking.

Tatum whipped her head around and glared at me. "While I appreciate the offer, I think it's best if we keep the number of people in and out of the safe house to the absolute minimum."

I reached down and adjusted myself. The way she responded to any mention of Kennedy made my dick rock hard every damn time.

Her eyes flicked to my crotch, and her glare

morphed into a smirk. Shaking her head, she turned back to Luke, "Let's get this show on the road."

With the use of staff elevators, back hallways, and rear entrances, Adrianna and Josie successfully made it to the awaiting SUVs without any unwanted attention. As an extra precaution, Josie and Adrianna were put into separate vehicles leaving Tatum unsure of who to ride with.

I stepped up behind her and pulled her against my chest. "You're riding with me," I said low enough for only her to hear and dropped a kiss to the skin right below her ear.

She shook her head. "It's part of my job. I have to go with them."

"Hey, Luke," I called.

He glanced over and made a shooing motion with his hand. "Yeah, yeah, go with him. See you in a bit," he said and closed the door. Seconds later, the SUVs pulled out of the parking lot, leaving Tatum standing there with her mouth hanging open.

"How am I going to ride with you? We flew here in a helicopter."

I pointed to the bike parked a few yards behind where we were standing. "That's how."

"That's not your bike."

I smiled at her initial response. "No, it's not. The mother chapter of the Blackwings isn't too far from here. Phoenix keeps a few loaner bikes on hand for situations just like this. Anything else?"

"No, I guess not," she said and turned to walk to the bike.

She picked up the helmet resting on her seat, but I stopped her before she could pull it on over her head. Grabbing her by her waist, I yanked her to me and covered her mouth with mine, kissing her the way I'd fucking needed to since the moment I laid eyes on her after Shaker put his bird on the ground at the airstrip.

When I finally released her, I turned without a word, pulled on my own helmet, and climbed on the bike. She slid into place behind me and wrapped her arms around me. Just before the engine roared to life, she said, "I fucking love you, too."

With that, I revved the engine and pulled out onto the road. It would take us around two hours to get back to Devil Springs, and I planned on enjoying every second of the ride.

We rode in silence for thirty minutes or so

before I turned on the Bluetooth connection in our helmets. "You doing okay?" I asked and felt her flinch.

She playfully smacked my back. "You scared the shit out of me."

I chuckled. "Consider it part of the payback you're going to get for scaring the ever-loving fuck out of me yesterday."

"You can't hold that against me. It's part of my job."

"The stunt you pulled yesterday was not part of your job, and you know it."

I felt her shrug. "Meh, it was, and it wasn't."

"You could've been killed."

"I know, and it's a risk I was willing to take. If we kept waiting for something to happen, more innocent lives could've been lost. Josie was on the brink of going stir crazy, and Adrianna was becoming more and more depressed by the day. I had to do something. And I knew exactly what that was after I went to see Luca—"

"You what?" I snapped and tightened my grip on the handles.

"Oh," she said nervously. "You didn't know about that?"

"No, I fucking didn't," I fumed. "When did you go see Luca?"

"Uh, it was the day I was working late, and then we went to the clubhouse," she admitted.

"Luke okayed this shit?"

"No. He didn't know until after the fact."

"So, you went by yourself?"

"Yes," she answered with a hint of petulance.

"What in the hell would possess you to do something like that?!"

"Because we were getting nowhere! And I knew if anybody could help, it was him!"

"Oh, this ought to be good. Please tell me how you got a mafia boss to agree to help the FBI."

She huffed, and then the little brat pinched my side. "Because Cristofano and Adrianna are engaged. Or they were when she was taken. She told us about their relationship, but I had a feeling she wasn't telling us everything. I assumed Luca would have fully investigated her background before allowing her to become a part of their family, and he probably knew things we would never be able to find. And I was right."

"You're an FBI agent! You should be able to find anything!"

"I fucking did, you big giant asshole!"

That was it. I was fucking furious with her and her nonchalance about putting her life in danger multiple times. I pulled off the road and into the first parking lot I came to, which happened to be a hole-in-the-wall roadside bar. Perfect.

Yanking my helmet off, I slammed it on my seat and walked inside without a backward glance. As expected, Tatum stomped in behind me seconds later.

I pulled a fifty from my wallet and held it out for the bartender. "Bathroom?"

He nodded in the direction of the restroom and took the money from my hand. I grabbed Tatum's hand and tugged her along behind me.

Once inside, I locked the door and smashed my lips to hers in a brutal kiss. While devouring her mouth, I undid her belt and popped the button on her pants. Breaking the kiss, I quickly turned her around and pushed her toward the sink. "Better hold on tight, sugar tits."

She gripped the edge of the sink while I yanked her pants and panties down her legs. Then, I landed smack after smack to her pale, pert ass. "You. Can't. Do. Shit. Like. That. Ever. Again."

"But it's my—" Her words morphed into a

low groan when I thrust my full length inside of her.

"What did I just say?" I gritted out, each word punctuated by a punishing thrust.

"Trey," she gasped. "Oh, fuck, Trey."

I felt her walls begin to tighten around me, signaling her impending climax, and quickly withdrew from her.

"No. Please don't stop," she whined.

I slapped her ass again and ordered, "Hush." Reaching behind me, I plucked a condom from my wallet and quickly rolled it down my length. Then, I notched the tip at her entrance, but didn't push forward. "I want to fuck the hell out of you and not let you come. Have you ride the rest of the way home with your wet, needy pussy rubbing up against me and grinding down on the vibrations of the bike. Then, I want to tie you to my bed and toy with you for hours. So maybe you'll understand how much you fucking frustrate me," I growled and slowly entered her.

"Is that what you want? For me to fuck with you like you fuck with me?" I demanded.

She moaned and pushed back against me.

I spit on my finger and ran it over her little asshole. "Maybe I'll fuck this instead of your pussy." When her cunt clamped down on me, I chuckled derisively. "Oh, you like that, bad girl?"

"Fuck, Trey," she grumbled and tried to thrust her hips back, but I held her in place. "I'm sorry, okay? I'm fucking sorry. I didn't mean to hurt you or scare you. I just wanted it fucking over so we could all move on with our lives!"

"And what the fuck does that mean?" I growled and gave her a few hard thrusts.

"With you! I want to move on with you!"

With that, I gave her what she wanted and started fucking her in earnest. Reaching around, I pinched her clit between my fingers while I slammed my cock into her hard and fast.

"Trey," she gasped and then screamed when her orgasm washed over her.

I didn't stop. I had a lot of pent-up energy I needed to get out. "Give me another one," I demanded.

"I can't," she panted.

Wetting my finger again, I placed it against her back entrance and carefully pressed until it slipped inside her dark passage. Then, I began moving it in and out until my finger matched the rhythm of my cock.

"Rub your clit for me."

She immediately complied and started mumbling incoherently moments later. "That's right, baby, give it to me."

When she reached her climax, her knees gave out, but I was ready for that and wrapped my arm around her waist to hold her up. Half a dozen more thrusts and I found my own climax, groaning loudly as I filled the tip of the condom with ropes and ropes of my come.

After a few moments, I asked, "You okay?"

She swallowed and nodded. "Yeah, I'm good."

Pulling her up and turning her around, I framed her face with my hands. "I love you."

She grinned, "Yeah, big guy, I love you, too."

When we pulled into the driveway at the safe house, it appeared as if we were the first to arrive until Luke stepped out onto the back porch, and he didn't look happy.

"What's wrong, boss man?" Tatum asked, seemingly not at all concerned by his demeanor.

"I specifically remember telling you to redecorate this place," he fumed. "So, tell me why the kitchen still looks like a giant fungus and one of the bedrooms still looks like the inside of a vagina!"

"You didn't show me the pussy room," I laughed.

"It's not pussy; it's puce," Tatum insisted with her hands on her hips.

"Everything in it is pink and ruffly. There's even a damn pearl mounted above the bed!"

"Sounds like a pussy to me."

Tatum elbowed me in the stomach causing me to choke on my laugh. "When exactly did you want me to redecorate? While I was guarding Adrianna and setting up the store? Or maybe when I was trapped at the clubhouse? Or when I was in the middle of solving this case?!"

Luke opened his mouth, but I spoke before he had the chance. "Let's finish this conversation inside," I suggested and ushered Tatum toward the back door. They were both starting to get loud and would likely draw unwanted attention if they continued arguing outside.

Once inside, she huffed, "Look, I know you want this place redecorated, but I am not the girl to do it."

"I can do it." We all turned to see Josie

standing at the entrance to the kitchen. She shrugged. "I was in school for interior design when I met and married Sheldon. As long as you don't want anything too elaborate, I should be able to handle it."

Luke nodded. "I don't care if you paint the entire place greige as long as the creepy, themed rooms are gone, including those damn dolls."

"That, I can do," Josie said confidently.

"Perfect. You two can work on the house while Adrianna is recovering, then you can get back to working on the bookstore," Luke declared.

Tatum groaned in discontent while Josie giggled. Suddenly, Tatum whirled around with excitement written all over her face. "Since they'll be here anyway, the bikers can help us!"

"Whoa! Say what now?" I asked.

"Splain, Lukey."

Luke narrowed his eyes. "What did I tell you?"

"Never to call you that again," Tatum sang and stuck out her tongue.

Luke sighed and pinched the bridge of his nose. "We'll be able to wrap up the investigation much faster if I don't have half of my team stationed here to guard the girls. I've already spoken with Copper, and he agreed to provide protection for the girls through Jackson Security."

Right on cue, Copper called to tell me about my newest assignment. "We'll get a schedule worked out for everyone else, but I'm guessing you want to stay at the house around the clock."

"You guessed right, Prez."

"I'll have Grant pack a bag for you and bring it over."

"Sounds good," I said and ended the call. Then, I looked up and flashed Tatum a wide smile. "Looks like I'm moving in, baby."

"Great! I think there's a mushroom apron hanging by the pantry if you want to get started on dinner."

I swatted her ass, not giving a shit that her boss was in the room with us.

Luke held out his hand to me. "I've been wanting to do that since the second day she worked for me." I shook his hand and chuckled while Tatum glared at her boss.

IT WAS A GOOD THING THE HOUSE THEY PICKED was huge. In addition to the three girls, Luke,

Grant, Coal, and myself spent the night at the house. Of course, Tatum and I shared a room, but there were plenty of rooms for everyone else to have their own space. The other members from Tatum's team—Dave, Jack, and Matt—spent the night in the detached garage where Tatum and Adrianna were originally staying. Luckily, no one had to sleep in the doll room, but Grant wasn't happy about staying in the pussy room.

Tatum said she needed to talk to Luke, so I went on up to the master bedroom without her to take a shower. While the hot water poured over me, I couldn't help but wonder what the future would hold for me and Tatum. I didn't want to let her go, but I couldn't leave the club either. They were my brothers, my family, but Tatum filled a void in my life I didn't even realize I had until she showed up.

I shook my head. There was no sense in debating the pros and cons. The only way to figure things out was to talk to her about it. Resigned to having a conversation I wasn't ready to have, I finished with my shower and got ready for bed. I was fucking nervous, and I hated it. Taking a deep breath, I steeled myself and opened the bedroom door, only to find the room empty. Partially disappointed and partially relieved, I dropped onto the bed and closed my eyes, falling into a deep sleep in mere minutes.

TATUM

TREY WAS SOUND ASLEEP WHEN I FINALLY MADE IT to the bedroom. After a quick shower, I climbed into bed beside him and took a few minutes to admire his handsome face. The ever-present lines of tension around his eyes were gone, and for the first time since I'd met him, he seemed to be at peace. I closed my eyes and prayed the conversation I just had with my boss wouldn't destroy that.

31

BATTA

A week passed, and I still hadn't talked to Tatum. It wasn't for lack of trying. Every time I thought we would have some time alone together, something or someone interrupted.

As promised, Josie got to work on revamping the safe house right away, which meant most of my days were spent hauling shit to the dump or helping strip wallpaper and repaint walls. By the end of the day, we were both too exhausted to do anything other than fall into bed and sleep.

Finally, I had my chance. Grant and Coal were taking a load of crap to the dump, and Josie was helping Adrianna with a shower. The very second I opened my mouth to call Tatum into the living room, my cell phone rang.

Cursing under my breath, I yanked it from my pocket and didn't bother to look at the screen. "What?" I snapped.

"Need you at the clubhouse. Now," Copper rumbled and disconnected the call.

I grunted in frustration and stomped down the stairs only to realize I couldn't leave the girls alone. Pulling out my phone, I tapped the screen to call Copper back when Grant and Coal walked through the back door.

"Copper called and told us to come back," Coal said, answering my unasked question.

"What the fuck is going on now?" I grumbled and went in search of Tatum. She was right where I left her, painting the walls of the pussy room. "I gotta run to the clubhouse," I said and placed a quick kiss on her lips.

"Everything okay?"

"Don't know. Copper didn't share any details," I said, and then added, "Coal and Grant are downstairs."

She nodded and continued with her task. "Okay, see you when you get back."

I didn't give much thought to her odd response as I was too focused on what Copper could possibly need. For him to pull me away from the safe house, it had to be something serious. At that thought, I twisted the throttle and hauled ass to the clubhouse.

When I pulled into the parking lot, nothing seemed out of place, but deep down inside, I could feel it. Something was off. My suspicions were confirmed when the front door opened, and Copper stepped outside with a glass of whiskey in his hand. Holding it out to me, he said, "Drink it."

My stomach dropped as I reached for the glass, and my hand began to shake. Copper squeezed my shoulder, and I forced the liquid down my throat, refusing to acknowledge what was happening.

I looked down at the empty glass and wished for more, or anything, to dull the pain that was about to be inflicted on me. Copper shook his head. "Only one, brother. Let's go."

I took one step inside the door and stopped dead in my tracks. My dad was standing in front of the bar.

"Dad?" I asked in case I was hallucinating.

"Yeah, Son, it's me."

"Holy shit," I breathed and barreled toward him.

He wrapped me up in a huge bear hug, and I did the same with him. "How?" I croaked.

"That'd be me." I whipped my head around to see Tatum standing by the front door giving a little wave to the room.

I glanced between her, my dad, and Copper with a look of utter shock on my face. "You did this?"

She shrugged. "Maybe."

Dad chuckled. "Don't just stand there, boy. Introduce me to your woman."

Tatum made her way over to where we were standing and sidled up next to me. With one arm still around my dad, I wrapped the other around her. "Dad, this is Tatum Cross. Tatum, this is my dad, Jace Wild."

Dad extended his hand to her. "Pleased to meet ya. You can call me Bear."

Tatum shook his hand and smiled. "Nice to meet you, too, Bear."

Leigh appeared carrying a plate with a freshly cooked steak and baked potato. "Come on over here and have some real food, Bear."

"Well, you don't have to tell me twice," Dad said and made a beeline for the food.

I chuckled and followed him to the table,

tugging Tatum along with me. "I can't believe you're really here," I said in disbelief.

"Me either, to be honest, but I'm not complaining," he said and shoved a bite of food in his mouth. He groaned loudly and swallowed. "Damn, Leigh, I missed your cooking. You got any of your cookies back there?"

"Hey! Those are mine," Bronze shouted.

Dad laughed and wiped his mouth. "Some things never change."

"Seriously, how did you do this?" I asked. I couldn't believe we were sitting at a table having dinner with my dad.

Tatum cleared her throat and look down at her hands. "I don't want to tell you."

"Why?" I asked, immediately becoming defensive.

"Because she knows how you feel about lying, and that's exactly what she did to get me out."

"What?" I asked, not sure if it was directed at Tatum or Dad.

"Luke knows how I got the information that ultimately led us to Simon and Nolan, but it wasn't something we could include in the official reports. Since we were going to have to lie anyway, I thought at least some good could come out of it. So, we said your dad was helping us from the inside in exchange for a reduction in his sentence."

I grabbed her neck and pulled her to me so I could kiss the ever-loving shit out of her. "Thank you," I whispered against her lips.

Tatum stayed for an hour or two before she had to get back to the safe house, but I spent the rest of the afternoon at the clubhouse with my dad, shooting the shit with the rest of the brothers.

Suddenly, the clubhouse doors flew open and Ranger stepped inside. "Well, holy fucking shit. They said you were out, but I had to see that shit for myself," he blurted and started for my dad. They met halfway and engulfed each other in a huge hug, taking turns lifting the other off the ground while they slapped one another on the back. "Damn good to see ya, Bear."

"You too, brother. How you liking it in Croftridge?"

They moved over to where the pool tables were set up and started a game as they continued to chat.

"You better find a way to keep that woman," Copper said from my side.

"I'm going to give it my best shot," I vowed.

IT WAS WELL AFTER MIDNIGHT WHEN I FINALLY left the clubhouse. I would have stayed longer, but Dad threatened to kick my ass in front of everyone if I didn't let his old ass get some sleep.

When I opened the door and stepped into the kitchen, I was surprised to find Tatum sitting at the table with a steaming mug in front of her.

"What's that?"

She smiled. "I've always called it angel milk. It's just warm milk, some sugar, and a little bit of vanilla. My mom used to make it for me when I was younger and couldn't sleep."

"You having trouble falling asleep?"

She nodded and looked down at her cup, and it was obvious something was troubling her.

"You want to talk about it?"

She cleared her throat and met my eyes. "I made a decision today. I should've talked to you about it, but I didn't, and what's done is done."

My muscles tensed, but I forced myself to remain calm. "What decision did you make?"

"I accepted the new job Luke offered me."

I pushed back from the table and got to my feet. "You did what?" I bellowed. "What new job?"

She crossed her arms over her chest and smirked at me. "Overseeing the new division of the program that helps people who have been in protective custody transition into a new life. Your dad is going to be working with me too, as part of his 're-entry' program."

"Cut the shit, Tatum. What are you saying?" I growled.

"I'm going to be running the bookstore and this house—"

I was on her before she could finish, smothering her lips with mine. I pulled back long enough to demand, "Say it. Tell me you're staying here."

"I'm staying here."

"You're going to marry me and be my Old Lady," I declared as I scooped her into my arms and carried her upstairs.

"Only if you put a ring on it," she laughed, followed by a yelp when I slapped her ass.

32

BATTA

Riding down the road with my Dad on his bike beside me should have been one of the happiest moments of my life. But it wasn't. Because of where we were going.

I pulled into a driveway I'd only been in one other time in the last thirteen years. And it was just as heart-wrenching and nausea-inducing as it was the last time.

"Dad," I croaked. "I don't think I can do this."

He turned around and studied me for a few seconds before he walked back down the front steps and engulfed me in a bear hug. "You don't have to do anything you don't want to. If you don't want to come inside, that's okay. But I do want to go in there. Your mother and I made lots of good memories inside those walls, and I want to go inside and recall as many of them as I can."

I swallowed thickly. "Go on in. I'm going to stay out here for a few more minutes." With a reassuring squeeze to my shoulder, he walked through the front door and left me standing in the yard.

I started to pace. It was just a house. Why couldn't I go inside? Logically, I knew the pain of losing Mom wouldn't change based on my physical location. But something held me back.

I don't know how long I had been pacing the length of the front yard when the sound of a vehicle pulling into the driveway caught my attention. I looked up to see Tatum hopping out of her truck.

"What're you doing here?"

She didn't say anything as she approached with something cradled in her arms. When she got closer, she held out a stuffed pig to me. "This is Mr. Piggles's girlfriend Petunia." She wiggled her hand. "Take her."

I took the pig from her outstretched hand and studied it. The fur was faded and probably in need of a washing, but you could clearly tell Petunia had seen a lot of love in her life.

"When my mother realized how attached I'd become to Mr. Piggles, she went out and bought another one to have on hand in case anything happened to him. After four or five years of hiding it in her closet, Mom finally told me what she'd done and let me have the replacement pig. I immediately named her Petunia and deemed her Mr. Piggles's girlfriend."

"Okay…"

She stared at the stuffed pig in my hands with a fondness in her eyes. "While I loved Petunia the moment she was given to me, she wasn't Mr. Piggles, even though by all accounts, she is the same."

It wasn't like Tatum to beat around the bush or wax on poetically. "What're you getting at?"

"You're afraid to walk into that house because you think it'll be the same as it was when you used to walk through the door. And, technically, it is the same house, but it's not the same home. Go inside with your dad. Miss your mom with him. Help him make it a home again."

I looked down at my feet and rubbed the toe of my boot in the dirt. "Fuck," I sniffed.

Her hands landed on my cheeks and she tilted my head enough so she could see my eyes. "I love you. And I'll be waiting for you at *our* home." With that, she turned and went back to her truck.

Once she was gone, I squeezed the pig to my chest. "All right, Petunia, let's do this."

EPILOGUE

TATUM

Three Months Later

"Are you sure about this?" I asked Adrianna.

She smiled and nodded. "One-hundred-percent."

"You know you'll always have a place here with us if you ever need it," I told her for the hundredth time.

She pulled me in for a tight hug. "I know. And that means more to me than you'll ever know."

I exhaled slowly and tried to fight back the tears. The investigation was complete. Even though her father and his partners were still awaiting trial, we determined she was no longer in danger when Sheldon finally admitted that he only took her to get back at her and Cristofano and never actually had a buyer for her organs. So, she was leaving, going back to the life she had before all this began. And I was going to miss her like crazy.

"I wish you would at least let me drive you."

She squeezed me even tighter. "It's not that I don't want you to, but I need to do this on my own."

"I know," I whispered. Inhaling deeply, I let her go and stepped back. Josie sidled up next to me and slid her arm around my waist. Together, we watched as the hired car drove away with Adrianna.

"Fuck," I sniffed and wiped an errant tear from my cheek. "Will it always be this hard?"

Josie rested her head on my shoulder. "It probably won't be easy to let the others go, but Adrianna was special."

"Yeah, she was," I said solemnly and sniffed again.

"Come on, Tay-Tay, she's not that far away. We'll still get to see her," Josie said, trying to cheer me up.

I smiled and turned to face my younger sister. "At least you're not leaving me." After completely overhauling the entire safe house, Josie decided that interior decorating wasn't how she wanted to spend the rest of her life and asked if she could stay and help with the house and the bookstore. It took some finagling, and me being a complete pain in the ass, but Luke finally agreed to hire Josie after she completed the training he deemed required for the job—which she had just done.

"All right, that's it," Josie said firmly. "I wasn't going to do this, but you've left me no choice." Then, she took off for the back porch and pulled a Nerf Blaster from behind a flowerpot.

"Don't you dare!" I yelled.

"Or what?" she shouted back and stuck out her tongue. Then, she proceeded to blast me with dart after dart while cackling like a loon.

I shielded myself with my hand and took off after her. "You better run!"

Taking the steps two at a time, I was headed for the door when Trey stepped in front of me. "Move, big man!"

"Oh, my bad. I thought you might want this," he said casually and pulled another blaster from behind his back.

“I’ll fuck you for this later,” I promised and snatched the blaster from his hands.

Before long, Trey, along with Grant and Coal, had joined the fun with their own blasters. The house quickly turned into an all-out war zone. At least, until I ran out of ammo.

Tossing my gun to the side, I snuck up on Trey and took his blaster from him, firing shots at him over my shoulder as I ran as fast as I could. I glanced back one time and was surprised to see he wasn’t chasing after me.

When I turned back around, he was in front of me. “No!” I screamed and quickly pivoted to run the other way. But, I wasn’t fast enough. He wrapped his arms around me and gripped the blaster, trying to pry it from my hands as I continued moving forward.

Suddenly, we both went down. I fell forward into the coffee table with Trey coming down on top of me. Somehow, the blaster ended slamming crosswise into my neck while I felt and heard a snap in my hand.

“Shit, baby, are you okay?” Trey asked as he quickly moved off of me.

I wanted to answer him, to tell him that I wasn’t sure, but I was focused on trying to breathe correctly. I couldn't breathe, in or out, and it was starting to really freak me out. With my head on the floor and my hands gripping my neck, I started to kick my feet in frustration.

Trey got down on the floor and put his face right beside mine. "Calm down," he said firmly. "Try to swallow, then inhale through your nose."

I shook my head frantically, already knowing I couldn't swallow. "Don't think about it. Just do it," he barked.

I swallowed.

And then I inhaled a lungful of much needed air.

"That's it. Do it again," he said softly.

"Fuck," I rasped. "Throat-punching is no joke."

Then, I used my hands to push myself off the floor and promptly screamed in pain. I looked down and almost threw up. "Look at my fucking finger!"

"Oh, shit," Trey blurted and jumped up. "Now, remember, pain is temporary."

"Oh, shut up!"

"Come on, sugar tits. We need to go to the hospital."

"No!" I shouted.

"What's going on?" Josie asked as she rounded the corner.

"Your sister broke her finger and is refusing to go to the hospital."

Josie gasped and came over to see for herself. "Eww!" she screeched. "You have to get that fixed!"

"No, I'm not going to the hospital for a broken finger."

"That's your trigger finger," Trey pointed out.

"Motherfucking son of a bitch! Fine! Let's go."

Thirty minutes later, we were sitting in an exam room when my favorite nurse entered the room.

"Hi, I'm Kennedy and I'll be—"

"You have got to be kidding me," I groaned.

"Tatum," Josie scolded and directed her attention to Kennedy. "Please ignore her. She's in a lot of pain."

Kennedy blinked at my sister and then glanced at me. Then back to my sister. "Oh, um, uh…"

"Any chance River is here?" I gritted out.

"Y-yes, she is. I'll just get her for you," Kennedy stammered and quickly left the room.

"Would it kill you to be nice to her?" Trey asked.

"No, but it might kill you," I snapped.

"Knock, knock," River said and entered the room. "What's going on?"

"The big, bad Batta broke my finger," I said and held it up for her to see.

River's nose scrunched as she studied my finger. "He sure did. Let's go ahead and get that x-rayed. Follow me."

"I didn't break it!" Trey shouted after us. "Don't you put that in her chart."

River laughed. "Whatever you say, Bratta."

"Bratta," I repeated. "That's a good one."

After the x-ray confirmed what we already knew, my finger was put in what I called a baby cast and I was sent home.

"You know I'm going to milk this for all I can, right?" I asked once we were in the car.

"I would expect nothing less," Trey said with a wink.

"At least it's not my ring finger," I mused and studied my hands.

"Yeah, that would've sucked if they had to cut your ring off," Josie pointed out.

I glanced down at the ring on my hand. It

really would have sucked to cut it off. I wasn't much of a girly girl. I didn't wear much makeup, usually had my hair up in a ponytail or bun, and rarely wore jewelry. But Trey gave me the most beautiful diamond ring when he proposed. It was big, sparkly and super girly, and I loved it. From the moment he slipped it on my finger, I had never taken it off, and I hoped I would never have to.

BONUS SCENE

TATUM

"Why are we doing this at Leigh's house?" I asked my sister.

"Because she offered to host."

"But we own a bookstore. It would make more sense to have a book discussion at a bookstore," I insisted.

"Well, we're not, so shut up about it," Josie snapped.

I stuck my tongue out at her but kept my mouth shut until we arrived at River's house to pick up her and Avery.

Avery climbed into the back seat and quickly buckled her seat belt. "Please tell me you remembered the wine."

I snorted. "Of course I did."

"Thank you! Thank you! Thank you!"

"Everything okay?"

"I have a few hours without the kids. I plan to enjoy it to the fullest."

Twenty minutes later, we pulled up to Leigh's house. "Josie, will you grab my book while I get the wine?" I asked and picked up the bags of wine assuming she'd agree.

River knocked on the door. A few moments later, Leigh called, "Come in."

River pushed the door open and froze, causing Avery and Josie to run into her. "Ahhhh!" she squealed and covered her eyes while she burst into a fit of laughter. Avery and Josie had similar reactions.

"Let me see," I demanded and used my elbows to move them out of the way.

"Oh, holy shit!" I laughed. Bear was sprawled out on the couch in nothing but a pair of red boxer briefs and a copy of *Claiming Mine* by Amy Davies laying open across his crotch.

With his ankles crossed and his head propped in his hand, he winked and asked, "Are we going to discuss this book? Or would you like to keep staring at my nipples?"

Laughing, I closed my eyes and shook my head. "Do I even want to know why?"

Leigh came around the corner holding a phone. It was clear she'd recorded the entire thing. "Something about payback for replacing deodorant with cream cheese."

"Hey! That video has over seven hundred thousand views," I pointed out.

Bronze appeared behind Leigh and took the phone from her hands. "Bet this one will have more."

"Oh yeah? Whatcha wanna bet?" I asked.

"If I win, you have to dye your hair pink and wear pink dresses to work every day for a month."

My initial reaction was to scowl, but it quickly morphed into a broad smile as I held out my hand. "And if I win, you have to do the same."

"Fuck," Bronze cursed before he reached out and shook my hand. "Deal."

SPECIAL MENTIONS

Betting on Forever by Scarlett Black

Claiming Mine by Amy Davies

Elevation 966 Winery

Playlist

Closer – Nine Inch Nails
Bring Me To Life – Evanescence
Fighter – Christina Aguilera
Hemorrhage – Fuel
Supermassive Black Hole – Muse
Bartender Song – Rehab
Crazy Bitch – Buckcherry
Lips Of An Angel – Hinder
Sugar – Maroon 5
Always – Saliva
Without You – Hinder
Pain – Three Days Grace
Click Click Boom – Saliva

https://open.spotify.com/playlist/6LvIM8MUZFq3xN0pCgkFtE?si=ItFFSfAMQFGTdCelkEO-PQ

ALSO BY TEAGAN BROOKS

Blackwings MC

Dash

Duke

Phoenix

Carbon

Shaker

Blackwings MC Box Set

Blackwings MC - Devil Springs

Copper

Judge

Savior

Batta

Bronze

Coal

Standalones

Beached

Christmas in Tinsel Town

ABOUT THE AUTHOR

Website/Newsletter Sign-up
www.teaganbrooks.com

Reader Group
https://www.facebook.com/groups/tbbooks

Society6 Store
https://society6.com/teaganbrooks

facebook.com/teaganbrooksbooks
twitter.com/teaganbrooks1
instagram.com/teaganbrooksbooks
bookbub.com/profile/teagan-brooks

Printed in Great Britain
by Amazon

46381140R00205